ON EVERY TWIG AND EVERY BRANCH A SMALL BIRD WAS FLUTTERING
(From "The Chaffinch Tree")

DEAN'S
SUPERB BOOK
FOR GIRLS

PRINTED IN
DEAN &
41/43 Ludgate Hill

SON Ltd.
GREAT BRITAIN
LONDON EC4

Sole Agents for South Africa: Central News Agency, Ltd.
Sole Agents for Australia and New Zealand: Gordon and Gotch, Ltd.

Made and Printed in Great Britain
© **DEAN & SON LTD., 1964**

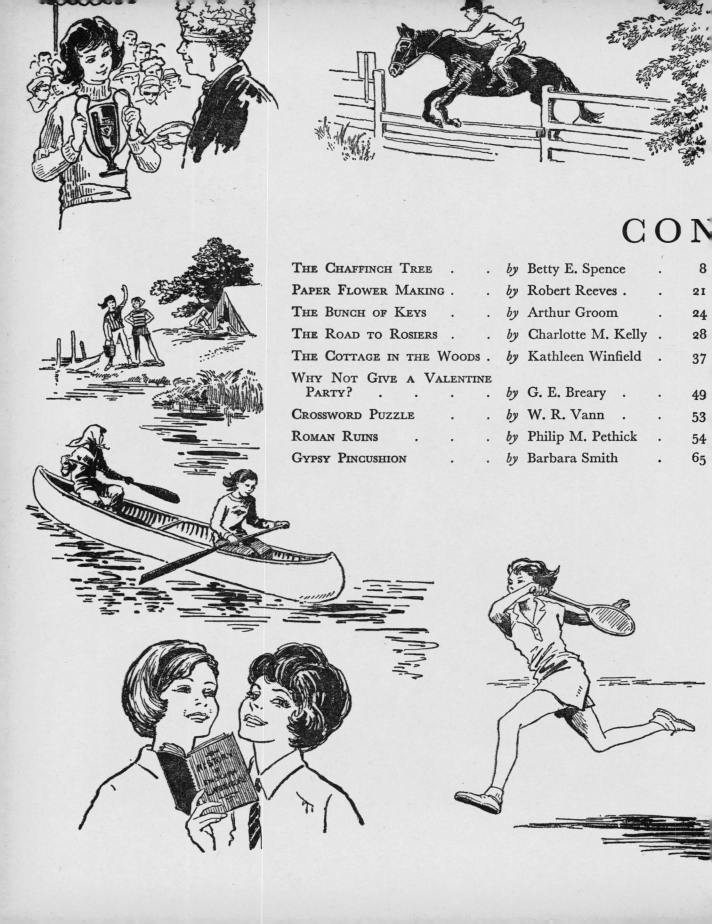

CON

TENTS

The CHAFFINCH TREE

by BETTY E. SPENCE

IT was the first time that Cherry and Susan and Jane had spent a holiday together, though they had been friends now for three years. They were all pupils at Woodgrange House, a small boarding-school that catered for girls whose parents were domiciled abroad. Both Cherry and Susan's parents were in Singapore; and though they lamented the fact that they saw little of them, at least they had their letters to look forward to.

Not so Jane. She couldn't remember her parents; they had been killed when she was a baby, and she had made the round of dutiful if somewhat reluctant relatives ever since. Holidays were always a problem where she was concerned, and now here was Easter looming ahead, and Aunt Clare, who always accommodated her then, was taking the waters at Harrogate instead—due, she had written, to an inconvenient bout of rheumatism. Inconvenient to whom, Jane had wondered rebelliously.

Now the three friends were commiserating together when Miss Lacey, their form-mistress, came upon them.

"What is this—a rehearsal for *Macbeth*?" she said. Then her cheeks dimpled. "That was naughty of me, but I declare, for very gloom you'd outwitch Shakespeare's three witches. What is it? Thoughts of end-of-term exams?"

The girls responded with rueful smiles. They liked Miss Lacey. She was young and gay and pretty and popular with the whole school. They felt they could unburden their hearts to her, which they immediately proceeded to do. Susan's parents were not coming home for Easter

8

as had been originally planned, and Cherry couldn't now go to her cousins', as there was mumps in the house.

"And Jane——?" queried Miss Lacey when the others' tales of woe had come to an end.

Jane shrugged indifferent shoulders.

"I'm used to staying at school during the holidays," she said. "One more won't make any difference. Last summer Aunt Lucy had to go to Paris on business, and the Easter before she had the decorators in. Christmas, Uncle Bernard was without a housekeeper so he paid for me to go to an hotel. Now I have heard from Aunt Clare, who promised to take me for Easter, and she isn't well and is going to Harrogate. That only leaves my godmother; and though she is a dear old soul—honestly, Miss Lacey, I'd rather stay here. And now that Cherry and Susan haven't anywhere to go, we at least can be together."

Miss Lacey looked at the three woebegone faces and smiled.

"Dear me," she said. "We must do something about this. We can't have you languishing here all through April— to say nothing of the caretaker and his wife. They do like to have the place to themselves sometimes. I think I might be able to help. No—I won't say any more now; I want to speak to Miss Jeffries first. But come and see me before roll-call tomorrow. I might have some news for you."

All three were awake and out of bed before second bell the following morning. They haunted the main corridor until Miss Lacey appeared. She laughed on seeing them.

"I nearly expected to find you outside my room when I awoke this morning.

Yes—I've got news for you, so I'll put you out of suspense straight away. Have any of you ever holidayed on Dartmoor?"

They shook their heads, wide-eyed with expectation.

"Then you have a treat in store. I have a cousin, a widow, who runs a small guest-house right on the fringe of the moors. I phoned her up last night to see if she could squeeze in three very self-pitying but deserving young girls. I kept my fingers crossed because I know how busy she is during the holiday seasons, especially with young people, because she keeps a few ponies for those who like to go trekking. Now—don't

rush me, I haven't finished yet," as Cherry and Susan, bursting with excitement, both tried to speak at once. "She said she *could* fit you in provided you didn't mind sharing a room, and I said that would be no hardship, as you were used to it. Then I had a word with Miss Jeffries, and she is quite agreeable; and, what's more, as she is going to Cornwall, she says she'll drive you down. Now all you have to do is write and get your parents' sanction. Well, girls—what do you say to that?"

What they could have said was interrupted by the clang-clang-clang of the breakfast bell, though the sparkle in their eyes was more eloquent than words. Later they raced along to the headmistress's study to confirm with her the part she was willing to play in their proposed trip. To travel all the way to Devon in the great Miss Jeffries' car—they couldn't believe it! It certainly raised their prestige in the eyes of the younger girls.

All it left after that was to contact their people, though they knew their permission would not be withheld. Jane's legal guardian was her Uncle Bernard, and he was so relieved to learn that she was going to be somebody else's responsibility for a whole month that he not only sent his consent but a substantial money-order to go with it.

"Gosh! Isn't he generous!" cried Susan and Cherry together when Jane showed it to them.

"Conscience money," retorted Jane with that closed-up look on her thin

face that her friends knew meant—"keep out".

By the end of term their spirits had reached a new pitch of excitement.

They had a whole blessed month of freedom to look forward to; and Devon in the spring, with violets and primroses blooming in the hedgerows, had been something way beyond their wildest dreams. But now it was coming true, and, what was more, the opportunity to go pony trekking made them the envy of the school. Only Jane had reserved ideas on that score. She had ridden once or twice but had never got the pleasure out of it that Susan and Cherry did. She didn't mind journeying along at a steady jog-trot, but when her mount broke into a canter she lost all confidence. She invariably lost her stirrups too; and on one occasion she even lost her seat.

Her riding-instructress had been quite furious about it.

"You should have kept hold of the reins," she said snappishly. "Now your horse has bolted for home and will be back in his stall before you are on your feet. When you are thrown from a horse you must *never—never—never* leave go of the reins!"

Good advice perhaps, thought Jane, but one that was likely to be forgotten when the world does a sudden somersault around you, and you clutch madly at space to save yourself!

But Jane didn't allow the trekking part of the holidays to worry her unduly, for when they arrived at Moorside House they found the ponies only a small part of its attraction.

Dartmoor was less than two miles away. From their bedroom window, on a fine day, they could see one of its highest peaks stabbing the sky like a jagged tooth. Mrs. Woods, their hostess, they found to be a slightly older, plumper version of her cousin, but with the same endearing smile, and easy, companionable manner.

She was always busy, usually in her kitchen, for the guest-house was full, but she still managed to find time to chat to the girls and suggest ways and means of filling in their days. Not that the days dragged in the slightest. At first there was too much to see and explore to cram it all in.

Primroses grew as profusely as buttercups; and violets too, nestling beneath their broad green leaves in the hedges. The thorn bushes were misty white with blossom, and they came home from their rambles with handfuls of arabis and campion and blue periwinkle, which filled the vases in their bedroom. In the open meadows they found cuckoo-pint and speedwell, the speedwell like tiny blue stars beneath the blazing glory of the gorse bushes. And on their quieter walks along the riverside they saw coots and moorhens and swans nesting.

It was a time of Nature's activity, and it stirred some deep longing in their being that made them feel that they must be up and doing something too. It was that same evening that Mrs. Woods told them that three of the ponies were free the next day if they would like to book them.

They set out early, with their lunch packed in panniers slung across the saddles. It was just right for an easy-going trek across the moors. The air felt like silk, and the sun shone as if filtered through a faint yellow haze.

"I hope it stays fine for you," Mrs. Woods called after them. "You never know in these parts. It can change so quickly."

It stayed fine for the next two hours. By that time they were well on to the moor, threading a way through open scrubland.

"Let's follow this track—it seems well worn," suggested Susan. "And then I bags we rest soon and have lunch. I don't know about you others, but I've developed quite an appetite."

"I hope we'll find our way back," said Cherry cautiously.

"That's easy. The sun is behind us now. All we have to do is turn and face it."

"We promised Mrs. Woods we wouldn't go very far."

"You don't call this far, do you? Don't be such a worrier, Cherry; and as for you, Jane—why are you straggling behind? Don't you like our company?"

But Jane was happy enough to go on jog-trotting along behind them in her own time. The sun was warm on her back, and Billy was a short, sturdy little pony who picked his way with care.

She looked about her. So this was Dartmoor. She thought of all she had ever heard and read of these moors—about their bleakness and loneliness and the swift, treacherous mists that suddenly swathed down to blot out sight and sound.

She smiled. It wasn't a bit like that today. The gorse bushes glowed as if tipped with gold, and the mosses and grasses and tiny, curled ferns unfurled to release their spicy fragrance to the sun. There were certainly no trees, except a few, stunted and misshapen by persistent winter winds. But looking all about her at the rolling, purple-misted moors she thought of it as a haven—perhaps the very last corner of England that had not been cultivated or commercialised. It was wild—but wild with a beauteous, unspoilt grandeur. She felt it must be the same now as it was in the time of Elizabeth I—perhaps even William the Conqueror.

She was roused out of her reverie by a shout from Susan.

"Hurry up, slow-coach. We've found a lovely spot to picnic in."

Indeed it was a lovely spot. A small stream, trickling down from its source high up on one of the tors, flowed out here into a deep, still, saucer-shaped pool edged with variegated reeds, and rimmed about with tiny marsh flowers. Susan and Cherry had already spread the ground-sheet and were unpacking their picnic boxes.

Jane dismounted and tethered her pony by the other two, where they could crop peacefully at the short, mossy turf. Then she saw it—the tree!

Just a rather small, insignificant tree— she did not even know what it was, as it had no leaves as yet. Its branches were misshapen and outspread but it seemed to be quivering—shimmering in the still light. She looked closer and gave an exclamation of delight when she realized that on every twig and every branch a small bird was fluttering. She rushed over to tell the other two.

"Come quickly and see. There's a tree over there with thousands of birds in it."

"Even allowing for exaggeration, I hardly see cause for such excitement," said Susan loftily, but immediately afterwards took back her words. The three girls stared in amazement as the whole colony of birds took flight and landed almost at their feet plaintively calling *pink—pink—pink*, that said as plainly as words: "something to eat . . . something to eat . . . something to eat".

They were exquisite little birds—some with pink breasts and others plain olive-brown, but all with white flashes in their wing feathers.

"They're chaffinches," cried Cherry. "I've seen them like that in my Aunt Alice's garden—but only in ones and twos before, never hundreds like this. See—the ones with the coloured breasts are males, and the plainer ones females.

How cheeky they are—and how tame!"

The chaffinches kept them company all through their meal, hopping almost within touching distance for the crumbs they threw to them.

"They must be used to picnickers," mused Jane. "I expect in high summer this is a favourite haunt with visitors."

"Then I'm glad it isn't summer now. I'm glad it's spring and we've got the place to ourselves," said Susan emphatically. "That may be selfish of me, but it's honest."

They told Mrs. Woods about the "Chaffinch Tree" when they got back to Moorside House.

"Chaffinch Tree—what a pretty name for it."

"Jane thought of it. And she's been mooning all the way home—we can't get a word out of her!"

In some odd way she herself could not

explain, Jane had been deeply stirred by the sight of the Chaffinch Tree. She could not stop thinking about it. It was almost as if it had cast some spell over her. It so preoccupied her thoughts for the next three days that Susan and Cherry found her dull company and chummed up with some of the other young visitors. A party of them with their parents had planned a trip to Plymouth to see the grand new shops that had been built to replace the old town destroyed during the war.

"They say there's room in the cars for us," said Cherry one still evening as Jane sat in the bedroom gazing out over the countryside with dreamy eyes. "It will be a whole day's outing. Susan and I said yes straight away. You'll come too, won't you?"

And when Jane only shook her head without answering, Cherry flounced out of the room in a huff.

But she had recovered her good humour by the next morning, and she and Susan waved excited goodbyes to Mrs. Woods and Jane standing in the porch to see them off.

"Now what are you going to do with yourself all day?" Mrs. Woods turned to Jane when the two cars were nothing but puffs of dust on the horizon.

"I was wondering if I could have Billy again today and go for a ride across the moor."

"By yourself? Won't that be lonely?"

"No. I'm only going as far as——" Jane stopped herself, confused, and

wondering if Mrs. Woods, as understanding as she was, might not laugh at her fascination for the Chaffinch Tree. "I'll go to the spot where we went the other day," she finished carefully. "If I could take sandwiches, I'd be back by tea-time. I just want a long, lovely, lazy day all to myself."

Mrs. Woods lifted an apprehensive eye towards the sky.

"I don't like the look of that veil across the sun. Still, it might clear away. If I hadn't got the evening meal to worry about I'd be tempted to come with you. It's twenty years since I sat astride a horse—but I'd risk it to keep you company."

As fond as she was of kind Mrs. Woods, Jane wasn't sorry that her duties prevented her accompanying her after all. She wanted this day to herself, and, giving Billy his head, they wandered peacefully, unhurriedly along the track through the bracken.

She became gradually conscious that the world had gone very silent. The birds had stopped singing, and, looking up, she saw the sun slowly engulfed by a milky-coloured vapour that seemed to be rolling off the ground in giant clouds. Was it a Dartmoor mist—one of those dreadful, clammy frightening mists she had heard so much of?

At first she was too terrified to think clearly. It wasn't until Billy whinnied and pawed the ground restlessly with his hoof that she realised he was as nervous as herself. Patting his neck to give him confidence helped to retrieve her own. She looked back, but a thick, white wall blotted out the landscape. But the track was still visible. She could see it through the shifting vapour at Billy's feet. The question was—to go on, or go back? When she decided to keep on for the Chaffinch Tree she told herself it was because the track led straight to it and she was more than halfway there. Even to herself she didn't like to admit that it was drawing her in some compelling way.

When she came on it at last, looming out of the mist like a crouching scarecrow with dozens of arms of different lengths, she could hardly recognise it for the same tree that just a few days before had vibrated with the flutterings and twitterings of hundreds of tiny chaffinches. They were there still—but silent now and motionless, the mist turning into drops of moisture that glittered on their wings like diamonds.

Jane dismounted. She was chilled to the bone, and wished she had thought to bring a sweater. Billy whinnied again, and she put her arm across his neck, feeling the warmth of his quivering sides.

How different everywhere looked now from when she had come with Susan and Cherry. The magic had gone—something sinister and frightening had taken its place. Even the silence was unearthly —"not a sound, not a sound in all this world," she thought; then stiffened, for there was a sound—a sound that she didn't at first recognise. Then it came again—a groan.

Jane literally felt the hairs rise at the base of her skull. All the old stories she had heard of Dartmoor came flooding back to drown her with apprehension. Ghosts—escaped convicts—hunted men. Then came the groan again, so loud it was almost at her feet. She couldn't shut her ears to it—or her natural feelings.

She called out: "Who is there? Where are you?"

And a cry came back: "Over here—for pity's sake."

Over here could be anywhere in that mist. Jane inched her way across the ground guided by the cries that seemed to be growing more feeble. Her feet found him. She almost fell over him. She was on her knees in an instant, staring down at the barely conscious man.

His eyes fluttered open and then closed with a look of pain that pierced to her heart. He had several days' stubble of beard, and his clothes were torn. She noticed his hands were badly scarred and bleeding, and on the side of his head blood was matted in his greying hair.

He opened his eyes again and made a gesture towards his lips. They were cracked and dry, and his cheeks hollow as if he had been without food for days.

He might be an escaped convict—it would account for his appearance and condition—but he was also a human being at the end of his tether. Without hesitation Jane fetched the water bottle from her knapsack.

She had to support his head whilst he drank feverishly. She offered him a sandwich too, but he pushed it away.

B

"Just give me time," he said, labouring for breath. "I'll recover in a minute."

Jane sat by his side and waited. A little way off Billy cropped at the close grass. From the distance came the call of the cuckoo—so somewhere outside this wall of mist the sun was shining.

And then before her eyes a miracle happened—or that was how it seemed to her. The mist rolled away, gathering itself into great shoulders of vapour and then evaporating; and sharply by contrast all the colours of the moor appeared, purples and greens, and soft golden browns, blacks and silver greys. But, best of all, the Chaffinch Tree came to life again. The branches quivered and rustled as the birds stirred and began preening

their damp feathers—then "pink—pink —pink"—they had found her out and were all about her, flirting, fluttering, giving their urgent call—plaintively begging for tit-bits. Jane laughed and threw them pieces of bread, and then the man beside her moved and said, "I think I could manage that sandwich now."

Just on the main road outside the village of Edgemoor, before it rose steeply to approach the Dartmoor ridge, stood a small round cottage that had once been a toll-house. In it lived a retired gamekeeper, and he was pottering about in his garden, spraying his roses, when he heard the slow clip-clop of pony's hooves on the road. He looked up and his pipe nearly fell out of his mouth in astonishment. As he told his wife afterwards, "There she were—a slim bit of a gel no bigger round the middle than that birch tree, and there were that girt load of a man, astride that game little hoss, and the man's heels almost dragging in the dirt. He was all in, mind you, an' how that lass managed to hold him on or got him into the saddle in the fust place is nobody's business. But there he were, and she had led him all the way like that from Mere Hollow, though she called it by some other outlandish name I can't think of now. Wouldn't tell me 'er name. Made off as if she hadn't any time left in this world, but would make me take her purse to 'elp pay something towards the expense of setting the man on 'is way!"

Jane didn't say anything about her adventure when she got back to Moorside House. She was still convinced that the man she had helped was an escaped

convict, and she didn't think she could face Mrs. Woods' horror or her friends' indignation that she had risked so much to rescue an outcast from society.

She tried not to wonder what would become of him now. Taken back into custody, she suspected—but she couldn't have done anything to prevent that. She tried not to feel sorry for him, but his face haunted her. Under its fatigue and pain it had looked a good, strong face. She was still thinking about him the following afternoon when she was startled by Mrs. Woods calling her to come downstairs.

"There's a lady asking to see you," she said, giving Jane an odd look. "She's in the little front parlour where you can be private." On a sudden impulse she bent down and kissed Jane's cheek. "You're a deep one," she said, then, opening the parlour door, gave her a gentle push.

Jane's heart began to hammer painfully against her ribs. She felt suddenly as if she were caught up in some web of chance that had started to entangle her at her first visit to the Chaffinch Tree. Then, meeting the calm grey gaze of the woman who had risen as she entered, her tension and uncertainty fell away, and she felt "here is a friend".

"I am Mary Hillman," the woman said, pulling Jane on to the settee beside her. She looked steadily into Jane's face. "Yes, my dear, I'd know you anywhere from my husband's description. David was in a very bad way when he arrived home yesterday, but not too far gone that he couldn't describe his gallant little rescuer in every detail. I don't suppose you knew at the time, but you had left your name and this address in your purse—that helped considerably—though David and I would never have rested until we had found you."

"Then he wasn't a convict," said Jane, wondering now why she had ever suspected he was.

Mary Hillman laughed.

"I grant you he looked as if he had been on the run, and in a way he had." Her expression clouded over. "He had hurt himself climbing. If you hadn't come along when you did—but there, we mustn't dwell on that side of it. No, David is a naturalist. He wrote *By Hill and Stream*—perhaps you have heard of him."

Jane's eyes grew wide.

"*That* David Hillman! We're doing his book for G.C.E. next year. Oh gosh—and to think I took him for a convict. You won't tell him, will you?"

"Why not? He'll only think you even braver than he does already. Oh, my dear, how can we ever repay you? You see—I wouldn't have sent out a rescue party for days. David often goes off on foraging trips, as he calls them—collecting material for his books. Sometimes he's away for a few days only, sometimes a week or more. He was climbing one of the peaks when he fell, and I think he must have been a little concussed. He had been without food and water for two days. He knew the general direction of the stream, and was crawling towards that when the mist came down." She smiled faintly. "He's well on the way to recovery now, though. He's begun to worry about his camera and other valuable equipment he's left behind—that's a very good sign." Suddenly she cupped Jane's face in her hands. "How I envy your parents—how proud they must be of such a daughter."

For the first time in her life Jane found herself speaking freely of her troubles—the loneliness of being an orphan, the feeling of not belonging to anybody. "And though Uncle Bernard, and Aunt Clare, and Aunt Lucy are awfully kind to me, I feel I'm an embarrassment to them. They just put up with me," she finished with a sudden burst of feeling.

Mrs. Hillman took hold of her hand.

"I'm a lonely person too," she said. "David is away so much, and I have no family. Be *my* family, Jane," she added quickly. "Come and stay with me whenever you can. Look upon my home as your home. Will you promise me that?" She stood up. "And now I must get back to my invalid. As soon as he is well enough he will come and thank you personally. That won't be long, and I shall be with him—so I won't say good-bye, my dear."

Jane was waving her new friend off when Susan and Cherry came in from a game of tennis.

"Who was that in that little green car?" asked Susan. "She gave you an exceedingly sweet smile."

"And you've got a look on your face as if you've discovered the riddle of the Sphinx," added Cherry. "What's up?"

Jane looked at them with a bemused, almost rapt expression on her face.

"Do you believe in fate?" she said, and not waiting for an answer: "I do—the Chaffinch Tree was *my* fate. Come inside and I'll tell you all about it."

PAPER FLOWER MAKING

by ROBERT REEVES

IT is easy to make paper flowers, and tastefully arranged, they provide an attractive decoration in the home all the year round (Fig. 1).

FIG. 1.

STEMS

Make the stems before preparing the flowers. You will need wire, around which a strip of paper is to be wound.

Place a 9-in. length of wire, $\frac{1}{2}$ in. from the left-hand side of a strip of $\frac{1}{2}$-in. wide green crêpe paper, 11 in. long (Fig. 2 A). Lift up the $\frac{1}{2}$-in. overlap, and stick it to the paper on the right (B).

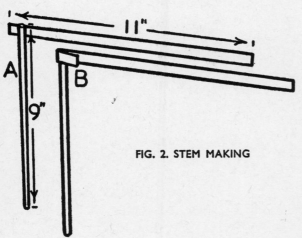

FIG. 2. STEM MAKING

FLOWERS
Rose

Use crêpe paper of different colours, 4 in. square—pink, yellow, red, or white. If red is preferred, then place together five pieces of this coloured paper (Fig. 3).

On the uppermost piece draw a circle $3\frac{1}{2}$ in. in diameter. With scissors cut the eight $1\frac{1}{4}$-in. slots

Then hold the top of the wire between the first finger and thumb of the left hand, and with finger and thumb of the right hand roll the paper downwards, until the whole length of the wire is covered (C). A spot of tube glue at the end will prevent the paper unfolding.

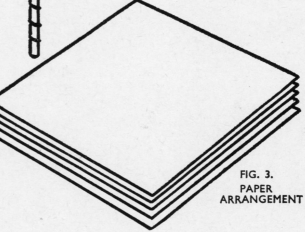

FIG. 3.
PAPER
ARRANGEMENT

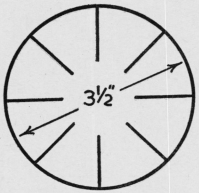

FIG. 4. CIRCULAR PATTERN

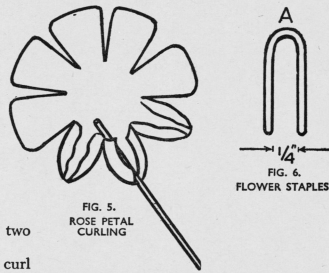

FIG. 5.
ROSE PETAL
CURLING

A

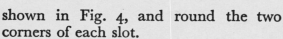

FIG. 6.
FLOWER STAPLES

shown in Fig. 4, and round the two corners of each slot.

Then, using a knitting-needle, curl each side of the slots to form the petals (Fig. 5).

The five circles of curled petals are to be fastened together with a piece of 2-in. wire, bent like Fig. 6. Twist a small piece of yellow paper around the top (A).

Push the two ends of the staple through the centre of the five circles, and gently squeeze up the petals to form the rose.

Twist the ends of the staple protruding at the bottom around the top of the stem wire, and cover with green paper to form the calyx.

Pink

Take a strip of pink or white crêpe paper, 16 in. by 2 in., and fold it in ½-in. sections. Then round the top as in Fig. 7, and fringe.

Open the paper, and it will look like Fig. 8. Run a piece of thread about ½ in. from the bottom, and use it to gather the paper together.

Work the petals to form the shape of the pink. Then join the flower to the stem by tying the thread tightly around.

Over the thread glue a small piece of green paper to form the calyx.

The fringed edges of the flower should be touched lightly with a water-colour brush dipped in red ink.

Chrysanthemum

The crêpe paper can be white, yellow, brown, or pink. Take a strip 24 in. by 4 in., and fold it over to make four thicknesses.

Press the paper tightly together, and with sharp scissors cut a fringe 2½ in. up from the bottom (Fig. 9). Make the cuts ¼ in. apart, and curl each petal with the knitting-needle.

Roll up tightly about 5 in. of the curled paper to form the partly closed centre. Then wind the rest of the curled paper around this

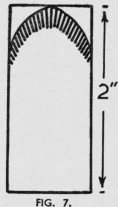

FIG. 7.
PETAL FRINGING

centre, and fix the end of the paper with a little glue.

Attach the flower to the stem with a wire staple (Fig. 6).

LEAVES

Artificial leaves can be made with green crêpe paper. Make a wire stem (Fig. 10), and bind with thread. Cover it by twisting around the paper.

Then cut out suitable leaves (Figs. 11, 12, 13), and wire them to the stem.

When placing the flowers in a vase, the addition of a few natural leaves from hedgerows will help to create a pleasing appearance.

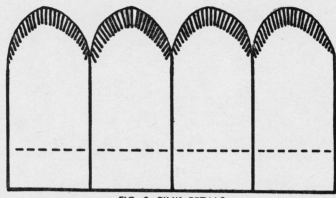

FIG. 8. PINK PETALS

FIG. 9. CHRYSANTHEMUM PETALS

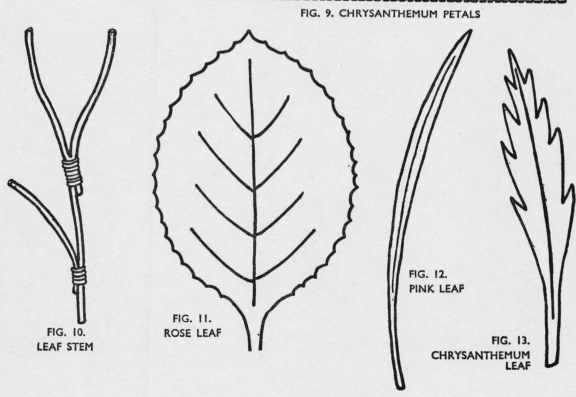

FIG. 10.
LEAF STEM

FIG. 11.
ROSE LEAF

FIG. 12.
PINK LEAF

FIG. 13.
CHRYSANTHEMUM
LEAF

THE BUNCH OF KEYS

Beryl and Susan had arranged to go to the cinema, but Susan had something else she HAD to do. "I MUST!" she said.

Beryl had promised her mother to clean up the home of old Mrs. Clayton, a very old friend of hers. In the end Susan agreed to go with her. "Humph!" she murmured, as they reached the house. "It looks a bit mysterious."

"Phew!" gasped Beryl after they had been cleaning up for a long time. "I hope your mother's friend is enjoying herself at that holiday home. THIS is hard work!"

But at last the task was done. "You know, Beryl," said Susan, as the two shook hands, "you'll make someone a good wife one day." "So will YOU!" came the reply.

It was while the girls were enjoying a nice cup of tea that Susan thought she heard someone at the side door. "Oh, you're just imagining things," said Beryl; "you always do because——" Then she stopped. "You're RIGHT!" she hissed.

Susan WAS right. Even as the scared girls looked at one another a man was trying the handle of the side door.

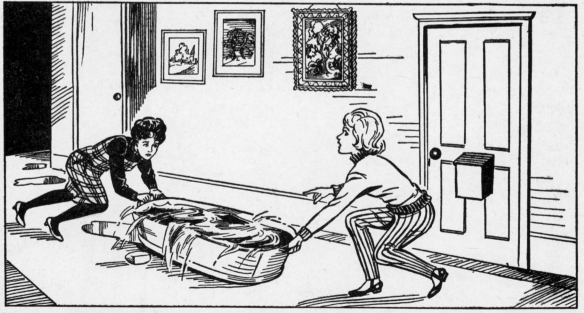

Meanwhile Beryl and Susan had recovered a little from their fright. "We'll take no chances," whispered Susan. "I'm not opening the door to ANY strange man at this time of the evening. And, if he is a burglar and tries to get in, then we'll be ready for him. Fetch that cake of soap, Beryl! But BE quiet!"

"I know there's no one at home," murmured the man, "but I must get in. I'll be more than usually careful."

"He's coming in," hissed Beryl in her friend's ear. "He's got a bunch of—er—skeleton keys or something. Gosh! I'm scared, are you?" Susan nodded. "I wish there was a telephone in this old house!" she whispered.

Then it happened. The intruder found the correct key and opened the door. A moment later his foot shot from under him on the soap and he went—SPLOSH—into that full bath of water. "What the——" he roared. "How dare you do this to me!" "Don't move," gasped Susan, "or we'll bonk you over the head. And these aren't modern kitchen things!"

"You stupid girls!" rapped out the man. "My name is Metcalfe—Detective-Inspector Roger Metcalfe. Here is my identity card if you doubt my word. There was a burglary here but it happened several days ago. I knew Mrs. Clayton was away and came to look for some clues. I found them all right!" Susan took the card he offered.

Even then Susan was careful. She had a good look at that card and at the man. "Er— we're very sorry," she said, "but, you see, you did act suspiciously, didn't you?"

Then Inspector Metcalfe had a clean up while the girls got a snack ready for him. "It was lucky Mrs. Clayton was away," said Susan. "She WOULD have been so scared."

The ROAD to ROSIERS

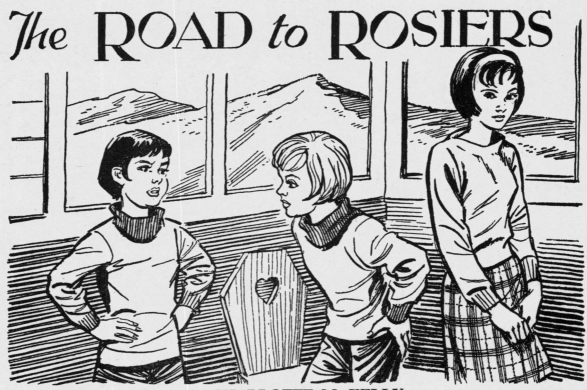

by CHARLOTTE M. KELLY

THELMA sighed as she listened to the heated discussion that was taking place between her two charges. It was one thing to come to this small Swiss valley, as she had done the previous year, for a holiday, with nothing to think about but amusing herself all day; quite another to be here as a "Mother's Help", expected to look after twelve-year-old twins, who had never been to Switzerland before and were ready to get into all kinds of mischief unless they were closely watched. Since her parents could not afford to give her another winter trip it had seemed wonderful luck to be offered this job, and she had accepted it at once.

But now she wondered if after all she had been so lucky.

"You'll find the children quite easy to manage," Mrs. Brett had said at their first interview. "Wanda can be a *tiny* bit difficult at times, but you'll love Kit. She is such a placid child, ready to fall in with everything."

Now Kit was saying plaintively, "But we went to the rink yesterday, Wanda! Couldn't we go ski-ing this morning?"

Wanda, dark as her sister was fair, tightened her lips in an obstinate line. "I want to go to the rink. *You* can go where you like!"

Kit pouted. "Oh well, I suppose we'll go skating. You always get your own way, Wanda!"

Neither of them had paid the slightest attention to Thelma, but now Wanda said casually: "You coming with us?"

For an instant Thelma was tempted to assert what authority she had, to say that she would start as soon as she was ready and not before, even to declare that they would go to the ski slopes that morning and not to the rink. But instead she nodded, and went to get her skates. Let Wanda bully her sister and ignore Thelma *if* it meant that the fine sunny morning could be spent down on the rink. For Thelma skating was the perfect sport. Most of her holiday the previous year had been devoted to it, and before she went home she had discovered the thrills and perils of ice-hockey. This year she had not had a chance to play, but she had been an enthusiastic onlooker.

As they were setting out for the rink they were joined by Delphine, who was staying in their hotel. Delphine had finer clothes and more pocket-money than any other girl in the village, and when she wished she could be both amusing and generous. But she was not as good at skating as she would have liked to be—which was perhaps the reason why she treated Thelma, whom she had met the winter before, with a certain coldness. Last year they had been equals, but this year Thelma was just a kind of nursery governess, her manner seemed to imply, and the fact that she could skate and ski far better than Delphine herself was not of any importance. Delphine talked and laughed with the twins, and even Wanda looked at her with wide-eyed admiration, while Kit clung to her hand. "I *don't* mind, I *don't*!" Thelma

told herself fiercely as she walked beside them in silence. But she did.

They were within sight of the rink, which was covered with flying figures clad in every colour of the rainbow, when Delphine spoke to Thelma.

"By the way, there is an ice-hockey match on tomorrow against a team from the next village. Joan Ingram is the captain of our team and she asked me yesterday if I thought you would play. But of course I told her that it was out of the question. You aren't free to do what you like *this* year! So she made up the team with someone else." She could not quite succeed in concealing her satisfaction.

Thelma went crimson with annoyance. She thought of all the things she could say—and she said none of them. But her expression was eloquent, and Delphine began to talk to the twins rather hurriedly.

That evening Mr. and Mrs. Brett, who were expert skiers, announced that they were joining a ski expedition to a nearby resort and would be away all the next day.

"So you'll be good children and do everything that Thelma says?" Mrs. Brett ended coaxingly.

"Of course we will!" Kit said obligingly, and slipped her hand into Thelma's, just as she had done with Delphine that morning.

But Wanda frowned and sulked, and insisted that she should be taken along too. When at last she realised that it was quite impossible, she did not speak for the rest of the evening.

"Can't you do anything with her?" Mrs. Brett asked Thelma. "She likes you, I'm sure."

But Thelma was anything but sure. Kit—yes; Kit was an affectionate little thing. But Wanda?

"Isn't there an ice-hockey match on here tomorrow?" Mr. Brett said. "You can spend the afternoon watching that. You'll enjoy it! Have you ever seen ice-hockey?" he enquired of Thelma.

She nodded but said nothing. She felt that she didn't want to see this particular match, but she knew that she would never be able to persuade the twins to do anything else.

The next morning Mr. and Mrs. Brett went off early with a party of friends, promising to be home soon after dark. Thelma was wondering how best to amuse two rather bored children when Joan Ingram came running into the hotel.

"I want Delphine! Has anyone seen her?" she asked. "Ah, there she is!" as Delphine strolled into the hall.

She smiled at the twins and gave Thelma a cool nod, before she said to Joan, "You look a bit excited, my child! What's the trouble?"

"Susan Lee has gone down with a sore throat and her mother won't let her play in the match," Joan said tersely. "So there is no one left to take her place but you."

Her tone was not exactly complimentary, but Delphine's face brightened, though she answered calmly, "Well, I'll play if you want me."

"I don't really"—Joan was too bothered to think of her manners—"but there isn't anyone else." She looked at Thelma standing with the twins. "If only you were free—but you're not!" If she had stopped there, it wouldn't have happened, but when she added doubtfully: "At least, Delphine said——"

At that, and at the sight of Delphine's triumphant expression, a little devil entered into Thelma, and to her own amazement she heard herself saying: "Oh, but I am! We were going to watch the match in any case, so if you think I'd be good enough for the team, I'll play."

"Good enough! You're better than half the team, better than——" Joan stopped abruptly, and then murmured, "Sorry, Delphine! But you understand——"

"Oh yes, I understand all right!" And with a furious look at Thelma, Delphine went away.

"Oh dear, now she is in a huff!" Joan said in a worried voice. "But she isn't any good at ice-hockey, and we do want to win this match. Be sure you're on time, Thelma!"

Thelma nodded, but already she was beginning to regret her offer to play. If Mr. and Mrs. Brett had been at home she would have no trouble in getting permission to take the afternoon off, for they were as keen on winter sports as she was herself. But with them away she was entirely responsible for the twins. How could she take a proper interest in the match and still keep an eye on them? But it was too late to change her mind now. Joan had gone off to the chalet outside the village where she was staying for the winter, and Delphine—Delphine—— No, it was too late.

"You'll be very good this afternoon, won't you?" she said to Kit and Wanda as they set out for the rink later. "You can stay near the pavilion and watch the match, and I'll come to you the moment it is over."

Kit smiled at her. "Oh, you needn't worry about us," she said. "Delphine is going to look after us."

"Delphine?" repeated Thelma. "But how—when——?"

"We met her just before we came out, and she said that as you would be too busy playing to mind us, and Mummie and Daddy were away, she would stay with us. Delphine is a lovely person, isn't she, Thelma?" Kit finished enthusiastically.

Thelma winced, but did not answer. Somehow she did not trust this proposal of Delphine's. The twins were a lively pair, and could be very tiring with their endless questions and unceasing chatter. Why should Delphine tie herself to them for the afternoon—unless she had some idea of getting her revenge on Thelma for keeping her out of the team? But how?

It was a smiling Delphine who met them at the rink, and Thelma's doubts vanished. She threw herself whole-heartedly into the game and forgot her responsibilities. An occasional quick glance showed her that the twins, one each side of Delphine, were obviously enjoying themselves. The match was going well for the home team and a convincing victory was in sight, when, ten minutes before the whistle was due to bring the game to an end, Thelma realised that the twins and Delphine were no longer in their places. She was not unduly disturbed—they had probably gone off to buy sweets—but when the match was won she slipped off her skates and began a search. She questioned several people who knew the Bretts, but they could tell her nothing. Delphine and her companions had apparently vanished into thin air.

Having made sure that they were not in the neighbourhood of the rink, Thelma hurried down to the village, deciding to look in the little cafés where she some-times took the twins for coffee and the pastries for which the village was re-nowned. She searched in vain at two cafés. As she was approaching a third, she met Louis, the ski instructor.

"Oh, Louis, have you seen the children?" she asked breathlessly. "I can't find them anywhere!"

"But yes, mademoiselle," Louis nodded. "They were with Mademoiselle Delphine down at the square a little while ago. They were looking for a sleigh to take them for a drive—to Rosiers, I think."

Thelma gazed at him in consternation. Rosiers, the next village down the valley, was where Mr. and Mrs. Brett had gone. What would they think when Delphine appeared with the children—and without Thelma? She could picture the scene: Mrs. Brett's surprise, Delphine's smiling explanation, the twins' delight at "running away". They would not care that they were getting Thelma into trouble—at least, Wanda would not. Little Kit might protest, perhaps. She was such a

nice child—but Wanda was different. One never knew what she was thinking. Children could be so disloyal, Thelma reflected. And then she pulled herself up. That was not fair. If she had refused to play in the match this could never have happened.

She was wondering gloomily what her next step should be when she saw Louis coming rapidly down the street towards her.

"Mademoiselle!" his tone was urgent. "There is bad news—I have just heard. There has been an avalanche along the road to Rosiers—one does not know exactly where——"

"An avalanche!" Thelma went pale. She knew all about avalanches, those great masses of frozen snow that from time to time become detached from the mountain slopes and slide down into

c

the valley, crushing and engulfing all that stands in their way. And the sleigh containing Delphine and the twins was somewhere on the road to Rosiers. "Louis, do you think——"

Louis made a quick grimace. "I don't know what I think. But we must do more than think. We must act! Excuse me, mademoiselle, I must get help!"

"I'm coming with you!" Thelma exclaimed, and despite his protests she stayed at his side while he raised the alarm, organised a search-party, and procured a large sleigh.

The sun was dipping behind the mountains as they drove swiftly over the frozen road that wound through the valley. At each turn they expected to come upon the avalanche. Thelma was sick with suspense. Would it be possible to dig through it—she had seen the men put several large snow shovels in the sleigh; and if it were, what would they find? She had heard of people existing under an avalanche for some time, but that would be in a hut, with a shelter, however flimsy, over their heads. What chance would one have in an open sleigh?

Then she heard the men's muttered exclamations as they rounded a corner and caught sight of the avalanche. A huge barrier of snow and ice lay across the road. Shovels would be of no use here; what was needed was a snow-plough.

Louis caught her frightened glance and shook his head. "I am sorry, mademoiselle," he said gently. "There is nothing we can do now. We just go back to the village and send for help." Then he added: "Courage, mademoiselle! They may be already at Rosiers."

But Thelma knew that he did not really believe his own words. They both knew how long it took to drive to Rosiers. Delphine and the children could not have got there. And if they had not . . . !

The searchers returned to the village, the bitterly cold air making them shiver. The sun had almost set, and soon it would be dark. Mr. and Mrs. Brett had said that they would be back "soon after dark". What was Thelma to say to them?

The bright lights of the hotel swam before her strained eyes as the sleigh stopped, and Louis said: "We will leave you here, mademoiselle. We have much to do."

This time she made no protest. Ex-

hausted with fatigue and anxiety, she stumbled up the steps and into the hall. It was empty, and, glad to be spared questioning, she climbed up to the room on the third floor that she shared with Wanda and Kit. She would wait there until she heard something—she shuddered at the thought of what that something might be—or until Mr. and Mrs. Brett arrived.

With her hand on the door of the bedroom she stopped short. She heard voices from inside, shrill angry voices: Kit's voice, Wanda's voice—and the voice of Delphine.

"It's the last time I'll put myself out for a couple of silly kids!" she was saying furiously. "I thought that you'd *enjoy* a sleigh ride instead of looking at that stupid match all the afternoon. I thought that it would amuse you——"

"No, you didn't!" Wanda cut in. "You may have fooled Kit, but you didn't fool me! I *know* why you suggested our going off like that without telling Thelma. You wanted to get her into trouble! You knew that if we weren't here when Mummie and Daddy came home *she* would be blamed! Well, I *like* Thelma——"

"So do I!" Kit protested.

"But you would have gone off in the sleigh all the same!" Wanda accused her. "That's a queer kind of liking! . . ."

Thelma decided that it was time to make her presence known and she pushed open the door. "I'm sorry," she said, "but I couldn't help hearing what you were saying."

The twins flushed and looked uncomfortable, but Delphine was completely unembarrassed. "Oh, there you are! I thought that the children might like to come with me to meet their parents at Rosiers. It would have been rather fun——"

"I'm glad you changed your mind," Thelma said soberly.

"Oh, Wanda had some silly idea that it would get you into trouble!" Delphine shrugged her shoulders. "She is such an odd little girl!"

"No, I'm not!" Wanda retorted hotly. "But——"

"All right, Wanda, I understand," Thelma told her as she stopped short. "If you *had* gone to Rosiers——"

While she was speaking the door opened quickly and Mrs. Brett and her husband came in. "Ah, here we are back again! My dears, wasn't it fortunate that we had arranged to come home by train! You've heard about the avalanche?" she said.

"Avalanche!" Delphine's face whitened. "What avalanche?"

"On the road to Rosiers! Just think, we might have been driving along it! Now, how have you all got on? Have you been good children?"

Thelma answered for them. "Very good! And Delphine took care of them this afternoon during the match. I was asked to play in it because Susan Lee was sick. I hope you don't mind——"

"Of course not!" Mr. Brett put in. "Our team win? Good for you! Can't let the village down, you know."

Mrs. Brett gave a sigh of relief. "So everything went splendidly!" She smiled at Kit and Wanda, who were looking very solemn. "What lucky girls you are to have Thelma to look after you! Thelma—and Delphine! What fun the four of you will have for the rest of the holidays!"

"Yes," said Delphine firmly, "yes, we will!"

The COTTAGE in the WOODS

by KATHLEEN WINFIELD

"THE trouble with you, my dear Sis, is that you have been reading too many thrilling stories," said Patricia kindly.

"The poor child is suffering from 'thrilleritis' in a severe form," put in Timothy from his perch in the apple tree.

"I am *not*." Jennifer stamped her foot. "There *is* someone there."

"Workmen." Timothy examined the apple within his reach with a practised eye. "Mr. Lorimer did say he was having some odd jobs done sometime soon."

"It wasn't a workman unless they've taken to wearing skirts," returned Jennifer haughtily, "and"—before her brother and sister could produce further dampers—"it wasn't Mrs. Lorimer or Mrs. Long, the housekeeper. It was someone old and she looked awfully cross."

"The sight of you, Jen." Patricia looked teasingly at her younger sister.

"She didn't see me. I haven't practised guide work for nothing," returned Jennifer with pride.

"A witch," suggested Timothy. "Did you see her broomstick waiting?"

Jennifer's annoyance ended in giggles as she sat down beside Patricia.

"Somebody from the village come to do some cleaning up," suggested Patricia.

"But we know everybody in the village and I've never seen her before."

"I've just remembered," said Patricia. "Mr. and Mrs. Lorimer were going away last Wednesday for some weeks and Mrs. Long was going to have her holiday in Devon. Don't you remember Mr. Lorimer telling Daddy about the Teachers'—or something—Conference?"

"I don't remember about the something conference," said Timothy. "I only came home two days ago, and men *work*!"

"So I've noticed," retorted Patricia, returning her brother's grin as he sat swinging one leg lazily from his perch in the tree. "Actually Mr. and Mrs. Lorimer have let their house to the Conference."

"Oh yes," agreed Timothy. "I did hear Dad telling Mother that repairs at the cottage had been put off until the end of September. Anyway, I expect Mr. Lorimer would want to be around while the job was being done. I should think that some of the 'something conference' chaps have overflowed into it."

"But they haven't come yet," objected Jennifer. "They aren't coming till Monday. There is no sign of life at the house."

Timothy slid down the tree. "Might go and take a dekko," he said kindly.

"Oh, might you? Not without us!" Patricia and Jennifer got up in haste.

"I believe you're just as interested as I am," pronounced Jennifer scornfully. "It's getting dusky, so we can see if there is a light."

"They could have let the cottage to somebody—it had got a little furniture in it," said Patricia thoughtfully.

"Before Mr. and Mrs. Lorimer went away Mr. Lorimer told Daddy that it was in a pretty bad state and they couldn't do anything with it until it had been put right," Jennifer persisted as if that put an end to the matter.

"Oh dear! Too much for me!" Patricia shrugged her shoulders resignedly. "And we shall have to bear the suspense till Tuesday, since Mummy and Daddy aren't coming back till then."

"Well, come on! It will be dark soon and we shall have Janet searching for us thinking we've been kidnapped, or 'poor little Jen will be catching her death out in that nasty damp garden'," said Timothy, realistically mimicking the faithful Janet who had been with them as long as they could remember. "Inspector Haydon and his two hideous lady detectives will investigate," he added slyly as he dodged the apple core Jennifer hurled at him.

Said Patricia thoughtfully as they made their way through the orchard, "When Mr. Lorimer inherited the Manor a few months ago he did say it would cost an awful lot to have it with the cottage as well made really livable in, and they'd only been able to do a bit to the Manor so far, but he thought probably his brother, Dr. Lorimer, might have the cottage and put it right."

The three proceeded across the small meadow, through the spinney and down the narrow lane that formed a boundary between their property and the Manor grounds. The lane led out on to the main road, but on their right a little patch of woodland brought them to one of the dividing fences of the Manor grounds, and very close to the cottage, originally for the coachman, not far from the gates of the old drive which was rarely used now, as Mr. Lorimer's uncle had had a newer, wider and more accessible drive made that brought one out nearer to the little town.

It certainly was getting dark, and as they reached the iron fence Jennifer said excitedly, "There! I told you so!" for behind drawn curtains in a lower window a soft light gleamed.

Timothy had just opened his mouth to make a reply when the sound of a car slowing down and the sweeping of its headlights as it curved to turn in at the big gates made them instinctively draw together, keeping well in the shadow of the trees.

There came two musical toots on the horn as the car drew up by the cottage. The three held their breath as the cottage door opened and a small grey-haired elderly woman—it was impossible in this light to see if she still looked "very cross" —appeared on the step. A man got down from the driving seat, went round to the boot and extracted a large square box from it. He helped the woman to take it into the cottage, and then from the roof of the car he unstrapped a bicycle and carried it in. Then, opening the rear door, he stepped inside and after a moment emerged carrying what looked like a human figure well covered in rugs.

They disappeared into the cottage and the door shut behind them.

After what seemed like hours to the watchers, though in fact it was only a few minutes, the cottage door opened again and they heard the low clear tones of the man's voice saying, "Whatever you do, don't let him out of your sight, and don't let anyone in," and the woman, just visible against the door, replied, "You need not fear o' that, sir." The man came down the step and got into the car, the cottage door shut and the vehicle was backed gently down the old drive and out on to the road, to disappear in the direction of the town.

"Ooh," breathed Jennifer, "isn't it exciting!"

"Well, it isn't our cottage and it isn't our land, so I don't see what we can do," observed Timothy reasonably.

"I know one thing we can do," put in Patricia. "Make tracks for home. We'll have poor old Janet in a real flap, thinking we've been kidnapped or something and getting ready to send telegrams to the parents. Race you . . ." As she uttered the last words she was off, her long legs flying over the rough ground.

"I say," panted Jennifer, "I believe *he's* been kidnapped!"

"Um! It certainly is rather rum," agreed Timothy.

"Yes, I suppose it is rum," agreed Patricia, "but, as you said, it is really nothing to do with us, is it? There! I said Janet would be in a flap!"

"And where have you children been? Catching your death out in that damp garden." This almost exact repeat of what Timothy had foretold was too much for Jennifer, who buried her giggles in the kitchen towel.

With one accord the three had said nothing about the cottage until, as they were having supper, Patricia said with apparent unconcern, "Janet, does anybody live in that cottage in the old drive? You know, it used to be the coachman's years ago?"

"I'd be sorry for anybody who had to make that a home as it is now," replied Janet, grimly raking away at the glowing fire where Cinder, the big black cat, was lying toasting himself on the hearthrug. "Why, the rain comes through the roof, and I've heard 'tis in a shocking state, though when Mr. Lorimer can get it seen to it will probably be all right, not that I should want to live in those damp woods," for damp was Janet's special bugbear. She bustled off to fill a kettle, and Jennifer exchanged a triumphant look with her brother and sister.

"I say—tomorrow——" started Jennifer, but Patricia interrupted her.

"Tomorrow we spend the day with John and Alison and Jane," she said. At any other time the thought of a day with the Grants, their old friends who lived a few miles away, would have been bliss, but this unexpected mystery so close at hand—"Oh! Can't we pretend to be ill?" cried Jennifer.

Timothy burst out laughing. "You can, Jen. It will be bed and lovely medicine for you. You can have my share."

"They are coming to fetch us at nine o'clock and Alison and I want to get that practice in for the tennis match." Timothy cut in to Patricia's words with, "And John and I are due for the rowing try-out."

"And you and Jane are going to clean out the old caravan," Patricia reminded her sister. "So unless we get up with the dawn—and I have a horrid feeling I shan't wake up—we'll have to wait."

None of them did wake up until Janet called them next morning, and it seemed no time before Mr. Grant and John were at the door. Mr. Grant put them down at the little lane leading to their house and went on for a morning on the golf links.

"Come and see what Mummy has given us for the caravan," cried Jane as she and Alison came running to meet their guests. Jane and Jennifer were off like a flash, and as the others followed more soberly John startled his hearers by saying, "I say, you know Sanders?"

"Upper Five Sanders?" queried Timothy.

"Mm. He's disappeared."

"Disappeared? But how—when——"

"Well, you know his people live in Wales? He was going to cycle home, thought it would be good practice for his French cycling trip. Reckoned it would take him two days. He was going to spend the night at a hostel in Gloucestershire. Well, he never got there! No trace of him nor his bike; and, what's more, you know he told us he was taking two uncut diamonds—looked like dirty bits of glass to me, but worth quite a bit if they were real—to his guv'nor. You know his *pop* is in the diamond trade."

"Crikey!" Thoughts, ideas, strange

possibilities, were whirling in succession through the minds of Timothy and Patricia.

"Promised to be down at the river by ten-thirty," went on John, "so we've just got time for a quick one at 'Ye Olde Summer House Inn'—guaranteed best soft drinks in the county."

"Soft drinks for soft people," cut in Alison unkindly. "I believe you made that up about Sanders—bit of practice for this super detective agency you are going to set up!"

"I didn't," returned John indignantly. "You ask Dad when he gets back. Come on, Tim, let's leave this odious female to poor Pat." But at this moment Mrs. Grant called John and Alison to collect some cakes that had just arrived from the bakers, and as they ran back to the porch Timothy took the opportunity to whisper in his sister's ear, "Gosh! Things are hotting up, but keep the cottage bit dark," and then they followed to speak to Mrs. Grant, and all four, laden with cakes, fruit and biscuits, were making for the summerhouse.

Patricia was longing to tell Alison of "the Cottage Mystery", as she termed it to herself, but, as she admitted afterwards, what with some other friends arriving for tennis and the general whirl of a busy and delightful day there was no chance of any private talk.

"Where's Dad?" John had demanded at lunch-time, only to learn that Mr. Grant had telephoned to say he had been invited to a golfing friend's house for lunch but would be back in time to run the visitors home after tea.

"I say, Dad, Bunny Sanders *has* disappeared, hasn't he?" demanded John when the time came, all too soon it seemed, for the journey home.

"Disappeared? I think that sounds rather dramatic," replied Mr. Grant, with a twinkle in his eye. "I agree he did not turn up at the hostel he was expected at, but there are numerous reasons why that could occur . . . Come along, young lady, you look nearly asleep now." Teasingly he helped Jennifer into the back of the car. "I don't doubt he has turned up all right, and we shall hear in due course."

But Jennifer, although very tired, was not too tired to hear the little exchange between John and Mr. Grant. Her mind as she confided afterwards to Patricia was positively whizzing on the journey home.

As they waved goodbye to Mr. Grant, Jennifer caught Patricia's arm. "I say, did you hear that about somebody Sanders?" she whispered, for this was, of course, the first that she had heard of it. Patricia nodded and put a finger to her lip as Janet, having welcomed them in, said that supper was ready.

"Supper, Janet dear? I couldn't eat another thing," cried Patricia, but Timothy managed better. "I should think you'll get fatter than Billy Bunter," said his sister as she and Jennifer, content with hot drinks, left him tucking in in solitary state.

While sipping hot cocoa in their bedroom Jennifer returned to the subject of the missing Sanders again, her eyes growing big with excited interest as Patricia, feeling that she could hardly keep John's piece of news from her sister, told her the few meagre facts she had gleaned.

"Diamonds!" breathed Jennifer as she jumped into bed. "Ooh!"

The next two days, to the disappointment and disgust of the Haydons, the rain poured down non-stop. Jennifer's one attempt to "go and post a letter" and evade Janet's vigilant eye was quite unsuccessful. "I'm not having you with one of your nasty colds when your mother comes back." It was most riling to see Timothy, oil-skin-clad, go cycling off on some affairs of his own.

"Why are boys always allowed to do things that girls aren't?" she demanded indignantly, tickling a complacent Cinder as he lay in his favourite place by the fire.

"Well, you are rather a one for getting things." Patricia looked up from her books. "I can't say I really want to go out in this, and now I must stay in I will get on with ye loathsome holiday essay," and with a sigh she gazed out at the steadily pouring rain.

Timothy had managed to have a look at the cottage on his trip, and reported no sign of anything except a bit of smoke from the chimney.

The morning of the third day dawned bright and clear, and the three were just prepared to go down to have a further look when the Grants rang up.

Jennifer, tired of waiting while first Timothy, then Patricia, then Timothy again, "fair talked that telephone to pieces", as Janet observed, slipped off on her own.

In a way it was even more exciting to be doing the "detecting" by herself, and she slipped along full of plans. It wasn't until she got to the little lane she realised Cinder had decided to accom-

minute later the cottage door opened and the little grey-haired woman came out and went round to the back garden. At that moment, to Jennifer's dismay, Cinder jumped down from the tree, strolled across the drive and in through the open door.

Poor Cinder had never been in and out of anywhere so fast in his life, and Jennifer realised that the little woman must have come in again by the back door.

"Get out of here, we don't want cats here," came in a tetchy voice, and poor Cinder was positively swept out of the cottage with the "witch's broom" that Timothy had teased his sister about. Then everything seemed to happen at once.

Jennifer vaguely thought she heard the voice of Patricia behind her just as the big car they had seen before drove in and drew up by the cottage door, but Patricia was her least concern at the moment. She could hardly believe her eyes, for there, sitting beside the man who was driving, was—her father!

For a moment dizzy visions of her father having been to the police, of the rescue of the boy in the cottage, flashed through her mind. But Mr. Haydon and the man at the wheel were laughing and talking like old friends.

"Well, I'll just have a look at my young man, and if you could then just give me an idea of the damage——" The man and her father were out in the road now, Mr. Haydon looking up at the cottage roof with a thoughtful air. Then

pany her. He quite often did, turning back when he felt he had gone as far as he wanted to. Jennifer loved to have his company, but today—cats were not like dogs. Dogs could be trained to do as they were told or kept beside one with a lead. As she made her way cautiously over the ground that smelled so lovely and leafy and woody in the little patch of woodland, Cinder disappeared up a big oak tree.

As Jennifer stood gazing at the cottage from behind the bushes the curtain at the left-hand end was lifted and a fair-haired boy, rather pale, about Timothy's age, looked out. She was just wondering if she dared to creep forward and make a sign to him, when the curtain was twitched abruptly into place again. A the cottage door, the only bit not hidden by the car opened, and for the first time a smile appeared on the face of the little grey-haired woman.

Mr. Haydon said something Jennifer couldn't catch. "On your head be it," returned the driver of the car. "You will certainly get a true picture after our recent downpour." Then they both went into the cottage and the door was shut once more.

Utterly mystified, Jennifer turned to see Patricia hurrying towards her, Cinder in her arms.

"I say, that man in the big car has just come and *Daddy* is with him!"

This bombshell was received with maddening calmness by Patricia.

"I know. If you hadn't gone tearing off on your own you would have known too. Mummy rang up just as the Grants rang off. Daddy decided to come back this morning, some important things had turned up at the office; and that man is Dr. Lorimer, Mr. Lorimer's brother. He was at the airport and was introduced to Daddy; and as Daddy hadn't got his car, he offered to give him a lift. Mummy stayed in the town to do some shopping and will be home at tea-time."

"Dr. Lorimer?" murmured Jennifer. "But what *is* happening? Who is the boy in the cottage?"

"I don't know who he is, but he certainly isn't Bunny Sanders!"

"How do you know?" said Jennifer seeing her carefully-built-up mystery dissolving into the shadows.

"Again, my love, if you'd only waited. Before John rang off he read us a price-

less card he'd had from Bunny, and apparently he hadn't disappeared at all. He got a bad puncture when he was some miles from the hostel, and pushed his bike until he came to a little inn, where they put him up for the night. They had no telephone so he couldn't let the hostel people know, and in the morning the innkeeper's brother gave him and his bike a lift to the next town on his market-garden lorry. Bunny got his puncture mended and forgot to let the hostel people know he was all right."

"And the diamonds?" queried Jennifer, still hopefully.

Patricia burst out laughing. "He hadn't got them. I should think that really was a bit of swank; he sounds a bit of a type! He put a p.s. on the card that took John a bit of working out. 'Banky advised sending dis reg. post,' and John imagines he told his form-master, Mr. Banks, who advised him to send them by registered post. It was certainly safer!"

"Oh!" Jennifer's face fell, then brightened again as she said, ever hopeful, "But we still don't know about the boy in the cottage, do we?"

Patricia grinned at her. "We'll have to find out from Daddy, and I think we'd better get back to the house," and she added warningly, "You know, I think we have been rather snoopy, even if it was a 'bit rum', as Tim said."

When Mr. Haydon finally arrived at his own doorstep near lunchtime he was greeted by flying feet and a bear's hug from Jennifer, who had been on the look-out for longer than she cared to think.

"This is very flattering!" said their father as Patricia and Timothy both ran to greet him too.

"Daddy, who *is* that at the coach-man's cottage?" burst out Jennifer as he put her down on her feet again.

"And what do *you* know about the coachman's cottage?" enquired her father, a mixture of amusement and re-proof on his face.

"We didn't really mean to be nosy," began Patricia rather guiltily, and between them the whole story came out.

"Well, well, I'd no idea I'd got a branch of Scotland Yard on the premises," her father said, trying to look stern. "The boy is Colin, Dr. Lorimer's nephew, and the doctor is his guardian, as his parents are abroad. Colin was going to join them for the holidays when he developed symptoms which might have been chicken-pox, especially as some of the boys at his school were still in quarantine with it. This put Dr. Lorimer in a quandary. He had not had a holiday for some time, and had arranged to go out with Colin and had already engaged his locum. He couldn't go to the Manor to stay because of the Conference, so in desperation he thought of the old coach-man's cottage, the bottom part of which was reasonably weatherproof. His house-keeper, Martha, who had been going on her own holiday, volunteered to look after Colin, and so Dr. Lorimer decided to give a hand at his surgery each day, and call on his rounds to see the boy. There you have it, my inquisitive chicks, if not in a nutshell—a very tame ending, I'm afraid, after diamonds and kid-napping!"

"So Martha looked so cross because she'd missed her holiday," mused Jennifer.

"Martha wasn't cross at all," said Mr. Haydon; "not with Colin, anyway—he's a nice lad. It was very good of her to stay to help."

"Has Dr. Lorimer bought the cottage, Daddy?" asked Patricia.

"Yes, and some acres of ground, and he is going to have the cottage repaired and modernised; but I think . . ." He paused, and looked at the three expectant faces with a little smile. "It is Colin and his mother and father who are returning home, whom you will have for neighbours. I had a look at the place this morning. Poor Martha had had to use a bath to catch the rain coming through the roof, but at least it did not get in downstairs."

So it wasn't going to be so tame after all, particularly for Timothy, who relished the thought of another boy in the neighbourhood. Fortunately, it proved not to be chicken-pox after all, but a chill with a high temperature and a slight rash—"which you youngsters scare your parents and guardians with," as Mr. Haydon remarked; and Dr. Lorimer had of course only isolated Colin until he was sure that there was no infection.

"Whoopee!" cried Timothy, delighted at the news. "Can we go and see Colin now, Dad?"

"But won't he be going abroad?" asked Patricia.

"Yes, but not until next week."

"Then can't he come to tea now?" Jennifer asked her mother hopefully.

"Of course, if he wants to," laughed Mrs. Haydon. So it was still quite exciting to go down to the coachman's cottage in spite of the ending of Jennifer's mystery.

"Who's going to knock at the door?" asked Patricia, as they climbed the fence into the old drive.

"Tim," said Jennifer so promptly that they all laughed. "He was rude about my discovery, so now he can do the work."

"Here goes," said Timothy and rapped on the door. It was opened not, as they expected, by Martha, but by Colin himself.

"I say, we're the Haydons," began Timothy, a little shyly.

Colin gave them a friendly grin. "I know, my uncle told me about you. I did feel a sissy not daring to poke my nose outside the door—didn't I, Martha?"

Martha, not looking at all cross, appeared from the other room.

"You had me worried out o' my wits, Master Colin. I never thought I'd keep you in once that temperature had gone down, but I will say you were not a bad patient."

"Good job it wasn't what we thought," said Colin with another grin. "Poor old Martha! I'd have had the spots, but she'd have had straws in her hair!"

Meanwhile Mrs. Haydon had been thinking about things. "I don't like to think of them all in that damp cottage," she said. "We've plenty of room here. Anyway, I expect the doctor would go back to his own house. Colin could have the room next to Tim, and Martha could have her holiday."

And so it was arranged for the week before Colin and his uncle departed for Kenya, and Martha thankfully packed her case and went off.

"What would you have done if it had been chicken-pox?" asked Jennifer of their new friend.

"Oh, lor, don't start us on more problems, Jen!" cried Timothy amid the laughter.

WHY NOT GIVE A VALENTINE PARTY?

by G. E. BREARY

WHEN Christmas parties are no more than a pleasant memory, and the Easter holidays are still far ahead, along comes jolly Saint Valentine, who asks: "Why not have a party on *my* day, February the fourteenth?"

And a very good idea it is, too, with lots of fun and plenty of bright-red decorations to cheer you up in the dullest part of the year. Even making these decorations is a warming business because everything connected with Valentine must be as red as possible. The first thing to do is to stock up with paper of this colour, paper of all kinds, tissue, crêpe, poster, blotting and gummed. You will need some white tissue-paper as well.

Cut out hearts and flowers; both help to create the right atmosphere, so here are a few suggestions as to how to use them. First, just in case your guests are the kind who stand aloofly about staring at each other when they arrive, here is a

GETTING-TO-KNOW-YOU GAME

Hand everybody a postcard and a small red pencil. Then pin on the back of every guest a red heart cut out of poster

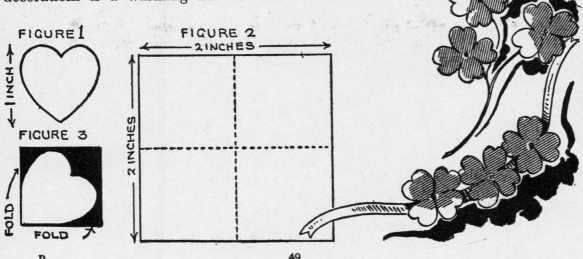

FIGURE 1

1 INCH

FIGURE 2

2 INCHES

2 INCHES

FIGURE 3

FOLD

FOLD

paper on which you have painted (in white) the name of a famous romantic character. There are plenty of them— Romeo, Cinderella, Prince Charming, Snow White and others.

The idea is for a player to discover, and write down, the names on the other hearts without letting her own be seen. This makes for a lot of manœuvring and fun so that shyness is soon forgotten. The first to make a complete list is the winner and may be rewarded with a

VALENTINE FAVOUR in the form of a flower bracelet or a flowery buttonhole.

To make the Flower Bracelet, cut some ten-inch lengths of white satin ribbon, which should be about half an inch wide. From stiff paper, cut out an inch-long heart shape for use as a pattern (Figure 1).

Now cut some two-inch squares out of red tissue-paper and fold them along the dotted lines shown in Figure 2. Lay the pattern on the folded paper, with the pointed end to the folds. Cut away shaded part (Figure 3) and open out into a flower.

Using two cut-outs at a time, make a large french knot in the centre of each with white silk, and sew them to the ribbons. Three flowers to each bracelet should be enough.

The buttonholes are made from the same pattern, but this time the flowers are fixed to wire sprays with Sellotape or a few twists of silk.

It is a good idea to have a little supply of these favours handy, to be given as rewards for competitions and guessing games. They will add to the festive appearance of your guests too.

Another game using cut-outs is called

HEARTS AND FLOWERS

For this the hearts are made out of red tissue-paper, while for the flowers white is used. Use the pattern you already have for cutting out the hearts. You will need a lot of these, so begin by folding a four-inch square of paper over and over, along the dotted lines as you see in Figure 4. You will be left with a pad of paper one inch square. Place the heart pattern on this and cut round it. This will give you sixteen heart tokens, but for six or more players you will need twice this number.

The flowers are made in the same way, using white tissue-paper cut from a pattern like Figure 5. You will need the same number of flowers as you have hearts.

How to Play

As well as the tokens, you will need a package of drinking straws and two small dishes. Divide the players into two teams, the Hearts and the Flowers, and choose a captain from each. The captains hold the dishes, the rest of the players each has a straw. The tokens are distributed about the room, in fairly accessible places. On the word GO, everyone runs off to search for one of his team's tokens. When one is found, it must be sucked up on the end of a straw, carried to the team captain and dropped into his dish. All this must be done without touching the token *or* the dish by hand. If, in the excitement of the game, either is touched, the player must stand out for the rest of the game.

The team that has the most tokens in her dish at the end of the game is the

FIGURE 4

FIGURE 5

HEARTS AND FLOWERS

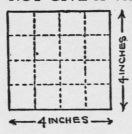

4 INCHES

4 INCHES

winner. Rival tokens, picked up by mistake, mean two marks deducted. Now for the

PARTY TABLE

Here are some ways to make your Valentine table really festive and gay. First, as a centre-piece, borrow a small doll and make a

Valentine Queen of Hearts

As well as being an attractive decoration, the Queen hides small gifts under her skirt, so she is doing two jobs in one.

Choose a doll which will fit into the top of a milk bottle which has been weighted with soil or sand, as shown in Figure 6. Dress the doll in red and white crêpe paper, making her skirt long and full enough to cover a number of small parcels.

From red poster paper cut as many heart-shapes as you have guests and write a name on each with white paint (Figure 7). Attach the heart to a length of white ribbon, using Sellotape or gum. Tie the other end of the ribbon round the gift

FIGURE 6

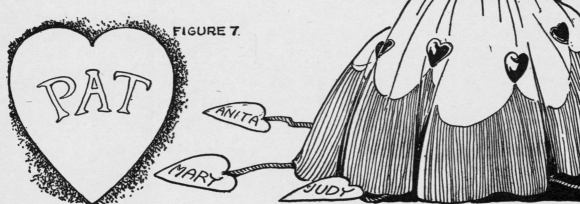

FIGURE 7.

PAT

ANITA

MARY

JUDY

you have chosen for that particular guest, and hide it under the doll's skirt.

It is quite easy to have food which will fit in with your Valentine colour scheme. Cakes, iced with white and decorated with crystallised cherries or sprinkled with coconut; ham sandwiches, using white bread, and, as a salad dish, small groups of

HOW TO CUT THE EGGS

SCARLET TOADSTOOLS

For these you will need eggs, tomatoes, lettuce, and chutney. Also a small quantity of salad cream.

Boil the eggs hard. Cut a small piece from the pointed end of each, enough to allow it to stand steadily. Cut a larger slice off the rounded end and scoop out the yolk. Mash the yolk with a little chopped chutney and the chopped-up ends. Add pepper and salt. Soften the mixture with salad cream and return it to the scooped-out egg.

Arrange the eggs on a dish of lettuce leaves. Place half a tomato on each and top it with salad cream.

You will probably be serving fruit drinks (as red as possible) during the evening, so decorate the outside of your tumblers with gay hearts cut from gummed paper and stuck on. Then, to save polished furniture from the drips, why not make some heart-shaped cocktail mats and stand them on any surface that needs protecting? This will please your parents and also add to the decorations. Figure 8 can be used as a pattern.

Balloons are a *must* for any party, as they provide fun as well as looking attractive. Bunches of red and white ones, red paper chains and some of those attractive Chinese lanterns, which are so plentiful and cheap these days, will transform any room into a perfect setting for a super Valentine Party.

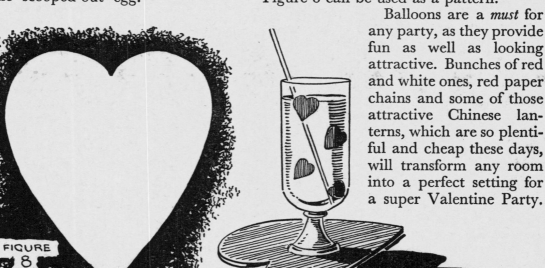

FIGURE 8

CROSSWORD PUZZLE

by W. R. VANN

(grid with handwritten letters: TAN, GEM, RED, TEETH)

CLUES

ACROSS

1. Look bright and well-polished (5)
5. Sat for photo or portrait (5)
8. Sun-brown (3)
9. Through (3)
10. A quick wash (5)
12. South American dance in 4-4 time (5)
15. Region (4)
16. Grammatical distinction between male and female (6)
17. Popular pastime with girls and boys (6)
20. Stayed fresh (6)
23. We hope your end-of-term one is good (6)
25. Dainty ornamental wear (4)
27. Deck up (5)
28. Nobleman's dwelling-place (5)
29. Animal mother (3)
30. Domestic pet (3)
31. Played about (5)
32. Keep them brushed clean! (5)

DOWN

1. Hat from stalks (5)
2. It is called "a woman's glory" (4)
3. Internal (5)
4. Woman (3)
5. Varnished variety of shoe leather (6)
6. Where to sit in beach-wear (4)
7. Way in and out (4)
11. Sort of hat with wide upcurved brim (6)
13. Girl's name—she seems mostly very good indeed! (6)
14. Precious stone (3)
16. Main point of the matter (4)
18. Did some mending (6)
19. Gay colour (3)
21. Waltz or quick-step (5)
22. Sleeping place on board ship (5)
23. Entranced (4)
24. Mount for 17 (4)
26. This probably matches the skirt (4)
28. Encountered (3)

(Solution on page 98)

53

ROMAN RUINS

by PHILIP M. PETHICK

"I'VE dreamt it again! We must look for those mounds today! Jeans and sweaters! I'll be around in a quarter of an hour."

The telephone line went dead. Pam Marston took the receiver from her ear, stared at it, shrugged her shoulders and put it down on the instrument.

"Ah well, I always said she was mad!"

"Cherry, you mean?" Pam's mother asked, coming from the breakfast-room, carrying a tray of dirty plates. "If you're going out, leave the washing-up. It's such a lovely morning. You get out while the weather holds."

"Mum, you're a dear! It's on cycles to find the legendary ruins to prove that this town was once a Roman settlement—or so Cherry declares. She's dreamt where it is for the third time—four mounds of nettle-covered earth mark the spot!"

Pam was still in her bedroom com-pleting the change into exploring clothes when a loud "Yoohoo!" and a trilling of a bicycle bell took her to the open window. She stared down at her friend Cherry Blane and at the long garden spade strapped to her bicycle frame.

"What's that for, you ass?"

"To dig with! Got to unbury the ruins, you know! Come on down, slow-coach! No time to lose!"

Pam went downstairs, kissed her mother goodbye and out the back door for her cycle. Wheeling this round to the front of the house, she was met by the demand from Cherry of: "Where's your spade?"

"If you think I'm lugging one about with me, you're more crazy than I believe you to be! I'm only humouring you by coming along on such a silly trip. You know as well as I do that there are no Roman remains in this town!"

"Correct!" Cherry replied, unabashed, the expression on her fine features showing no irritation at her friend's scepticism. "Historians note that ancient records indicate the existence of a large settlement by the Romans near here. It is thought that the Anglo-Saxons destroyed it completely, as they did many other places, and that the present town was not established until later."

"You may love history—I don't! Anyway, where'd you dig up all that information?"

"The reference library! Miss Chalmers declared that if I really intended to be an archaeologist, I'd better prove my capabilities by writing an essay during the hols about the origins of this town!"

"A kill-or-cure test!" Pam remarked grimly. "Anyone who could do that in the hols must be capable of archaeology! Still, where are we going?"

"My dream is of high ground, the four mounds near the summit, but nearby is a tower—any suggestions?"

"The fields near Barby—there's an electricity pylon on top of a hill there."

"It's not that sort of a tower—a stone one, or brick!" Cherry snapped.

"Oh! Um! Well! Ah, the field roads to Kreeby! There's high ground there and that derelict windmill on top!"

"That's it! I knew you'd get the fever in the blood. Right! Only three miles from here! I wish you'd bring a spade."

"No!" Pam replied firmly and rode out of the front garden to stop any further argument.

Riding towards Kreeby on the main road, they were soon out of town and, after two miles, turned left along field roads blocked every now and then by gates. The roadway began to climb, and the fields to the left rising even higher, until at last the windmill came into sight.

"There it is! Just as my dream!" Cherry cried, stopping so suddenly that Pam ran slap into her cycle.

The collision brought both girls to the ground and the grass verge sloped steeply down from the road. Neither could prevent themselves from rolling over and over. Their cycles crashed to the ground as they smashed into prickly bushes shielding a very wet ditch. Cherry's feet went right into the water, but Pam was a little luckier. She finished up with an arm in it and her face a few inches above the mud.

"I'll 'adain' you, my lad, laughing at your elders!" Cherry cried, hauling her feet from the mud and water with a squelch.

Pam pulled out her arm and glared at the thick mud caking it and clinging to the long sleeve of her sweater. Cherry's shoes, white socks and the bottom six inches of the legs of her jeans were likewise smothered.

"Do it adain!" the little boy ordered angrily.

Cherry scrambled up the bank. The boy backed away hurriedly and put the

"What on earth made you do that?" Cherry stormed and would have said more but for a peal of laughter silencing her.

She screwed her head round and stared back up the slope to the roadway. A small boy, perhaps four years old, was standing there, laughing with all his might.

"Do it adain!" he cried. "That was funny! Adain!"

fallen cycles between him and the irate girl.

"Wonder where he's come from?" Pam muttered, joining her friend. "Seems a bit young to be wandering around alone."

"Some farm nearby, I suppose. Had we better return him, do you think?"

She took a step towards the child, but he was not waiting to be caught. He turned about and tore off down the road,

his fat legs twinkling in the sunlight.

"That answers your question—no!" Pam stated, then surveyed her muddy arm and her friend's feet. "But what about us?"

"Yes, and why did you barge into me like that?"

"Because you stopped so suddenly. Oh, anyway, it's done now! Look, there's a bridge over the ditch down there. The water looks as if it's running fast there

and should be clean."

The mopping-up operations were carried out reasonably successfully. The bottoms of the legs of Cherry's jeans would have to dry on her in the sunlight, and so would Pam's sleeve. The shoes— once again the sun would have to dry them.

"Right!" Cherry declared some time later. "We're more or less dry—up the hill to the windmill. Those four mounds have just got to be there!"

"We'll be trespassing in those fields!"

"It's only grass! We're not going to damage anything. Come on! Wait— chain the bikes together with my cycle lock. They'll be all right behind this hedge. Hope the 'pop' I brought doesn't explode in the heat!"

And off the two girls trudged, Cherry armed with her spade and Pam feeling a little ridiculous. She shuddered to think what the farmer would say if he saw them!

The first field ended halfway to the top of the rising ground. A hedge barred their way and they had to walk some distance along it before finding an opening. Cherry went through first, a little careless in her eagerness to get to the summit. She looked back to urge on Pam, then let out a wild yell, twisted and fell flat on her face.

Pam, halfway through the hedge and bent double, gaped in horror as her friend started to slide backwards and disappear into the ground.

"Help!" Cherry shrieked, and Pam lunged forward, sprawling all her length but reaching out and grabbing her friend's arms outstretched despairingly on the ground.

"There's a great hole here! I'm in it up to my waist!" Cherry gasped.

"Don't panic! I've got you! Scramble out with your feet."

"I'm trying to! The earth's soft and falling away!"

The girls struggled for some minutes, then gradually Cherry moved forward as her movements broke more and more earth from the edge and it became a slope. At last her feet found a firm hold and she came out fast, stumbling up onto her knees and almost slumping down on the spreadeagled Pam.

For some seconds they lay gasping for breath, then both sat up and surveyed the hole. It was more than that, being a trench about three feet wide running alongside the hedge in both directions. The long grass had virtually hidden it from the hole in the hedge, for the excavated earth was piled a few feet away on the far side of it.

"What a death trap!" Cherry gasped. "Fancy leaving that for anyone to fall in! I can't even see the bottom from here!"

"It is on private ground," Pam pointed out as Cherry got to her feet. "Look out, the edge is crumbling!"

Cherry felt the earth giving under her as she tried to peer into the trench. Pam leapt to her friend and yanked her back.

"Do you mean to fall right in, or what?" she demanded. "Back through the hedge. We can't cross here, that's certain."

They moved on along the hedge on the safe side and when they reached the corner of the field they found an opening and a plank bridge across the trench. They stared down and saw that it was a good six feet deep and ran on across the next field.

"Someone's been after your Roman ruins!" Pam teased.

"It's for water mains to a farm, I bet! Anyway, we're still in one piece each, so up the hill to the mounds."

And up they went, breasted the top about thirty yards from the derelict windmill and there, just a little down the far side, were three low mounds of earth, side by side.

Pam goggled at them, then slowly it dawned upon her that perhaps Cherry had been working a big "leg-pull" all the while. She had found these flat, six foot or so square mounds before and had made up the dream to go with them.

"But she said four of them!" Pam muttered half aloud.

"Three or four, what's it matter? I've found them! Come on! Just in front of each is hidden a wall built perhaps over two thousand years ago. We'll be famous. The discoverers of the lost city!"

Pam was silent. Sun hot enough quickly to dry out clothing hardly seemed the weather for hard digging. But Cherry had no thought for that and attacked the ground vigorously. The soil was sandy and came up easily, a point emphasised by the crumbling edge of the trench.

"Cherry! What's the farmer going to say if he finds us here?"

"Thank us for making him famous!" was the sharp reply. "Here, your turn with the spade!"

"These mounds have no nettles and they look recent to me," Pam muttered, stepping down off the one before which Cherry was excavating. "These couldn't be Roman."

"What's under here *is*—says my dream!"

Pam took the spade and carried on the digging, but without enthusiasm. The hole was about two foot square and that deep in the centre when she struck something hard.

Cherry had the spade back and was making the earth fly in a flash. Pam stared incredulously as she watched something being revealed that certainly did look like the top of a stone wall. Cherry only uncovered the top two inches and

then started working along the length of it. After about a yard, the stone turned at right angles.

"There!" Cherry cried triumphantly. "The corner of a room. Look at the surface. It'll be stone blocks like huge bricks."

"Certainly looks like it! I never thought you'd find anything, but surely you're not going on digging without permission. I mean, we are trespassing!"

Cherry considered that statement, then announced: "You're right! Now we've found something definite, we'll see the farmer and get his permission."

"I'd like a drink. We left the 'pop' in the saddlebags."

"And it may have gone 'pop!' in this

heat. Let's go and see. Hi! Bring the spade. I'll have Dad after me if I lose that!"

They were almost back to the trench, when Pam suddenly stopped and waved her friend to be quiet.

"What's up?" Cherry asked all the same.

"Ssh!"

The sound came again. Cherry heard it.

"Someone crying—or calling out in pain!" Pam murmured.

"Calling for help, I'd say! But from where?"

The girls stared around them. No one was in sight. The cry was repeated, faintly, but somehow near at hand. They had been staring up the sloping field, but both of them swung round at the sound.

"That trench!" Cherry gasped. "It came from there!"

Without a word to each other, they sprinted down the rest of the slope. Pam grabbed hold of her friend and pulled her back.

"Mind the edge, you ass! If someone's down there, falling in as well won't help!"

They approached gingerly and got near enough to peer forward and just down to the bottom. There was nothing there, but to look along its length they would need to lean right over and the earth was not going to let them do that.

"How about going for help?" Pam suggested.

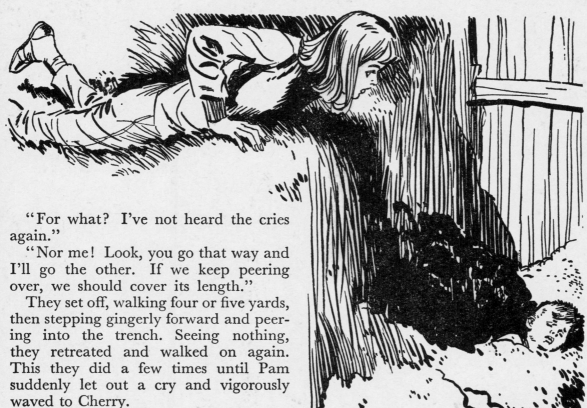

"For what? I've not heard the cries again."

"Nor me! Look, you go that way and I'll go the other. If we keep peering over, we should cover its length."

They set off, walking four or five yards, then stepping gingerly forward and peering into the trench. Seeing nothing, they retreated and walked on again. This they did a few times until Pam suddenly let out a cry and vigorously waved to Cherry.

But not waiting for her friend, Pam lay down on the ground and wriggled forward to the edge. Peering over, she found herself staring down at a mound of earth in the bottom of the trench, from one side of which protruded the head and one shoulder of a small boy. It was the one who had been amused at their tumble, but now his eyes were shut and his complexion deathly pale.

Cherry wriggled up alongside her and peered down, catching her breath in horror at the sight. "Is he dead?"

"No! His lips moved. You can see how it happened. Look at the edge opposite—the earth fell from there. We'll have to get help quickly!"

"Wait!" Cherry cried, holding her friend down. "The earth's still trickling down. Only a little more will cover his face. There's no time to get help!"

"We'll never get out ourselves if we go down there."

"One of us will—off the other's shoulders. Dig him out first, then get help. We'll go down up there a bit, in case we start another fall onto him."

They wriggled back from the edge and got to their feet, running a few yards before approaching the trench again. Cherry lay down and squirmed backwards to the edge, Pam holding on to her hands. Over she went, let herself drop and disappeared into the ground.

"You all right?" Pam cried anxiously.

"Yes! Slide the spade over. I'm out of the way. You stay up there and get help."

"I'll see if you need help first!"

Pam ran back along the top of the trench to the spot above the trapped boy, dropped onto her stomach and wriggled to the edge. Cherry was below, just starting to dig away at the earth covering the boy.

"There's more than it looks from up there!" she gasped out, shovelling the soil away behind her. "Not much room either! Oh!"

The handle of the spade had jabbed into the earth wall below where the slip had trapped the boy. With an audible "swish", more soil fell, smacking onto Cherry's bent back and flattening her to the trench floor.

Pam acted instantly. Slithering round, she let her legs dangle over the edge, grabbed the grass for a moment, then let go. She only dropped about three feet, but she landed heavily and stumbled back against the opposite wall. For one ghastly moment she thought that that was going to crumble and bury her, but only a trickle came down.

Then she fell upon Cherry, scrabbling the earth from her friend's legs, catching hold of her shoulders and hauling her up.

"Hurt anywhere?" she demanded fearfully.

"Winded!" Cherry gasped. "That was awful! Just like a huge hammer hitting your back. Come on . . . the boy . . . more earth may fall!"

Mainly using their hands and keeping away from the walls, the girls clawed the earth away until they felt something hard. More scooping revealed a block of wood about three feet long and inches thick. It was across the top of the boy's legs, pinning him down. Moving to get hold of it, Pam kicked against some more wood still buried.

"This bit of the trench must have been propped up," Cherry gasped. "Bet he tried to climb out by it, pulled it down on him and released the earth."

They cleared the wood away and pulled the boy out of the rest of the earth. Before going far, they felt for broken bones, but he seemed to be only bruised.

"Now you go up and get help!" Cherry panted. "I'm too blown. Climb up me and you'll get out off my shoulders."

"Sure you'll be safe?"

"I'll not move about, don't you fear!"

Pam pushed herself up out of the trench off Cherry's shoulders. She immediately scrambled to her feet and sprinted across the plank bridge to the other field, across this and to the bicycles.

Unchaining these wasted a few seconds, but then she was off along the lane, knowing she would find a farm sooner or later.

She found help very quickly, in the form of a man driving a Land-Rover. She met him around a corner. He stamped on the brakes and shouted to her, as she stopped and called to him.

"Have you seen a small boy wandering about?" he asked. "He's lost."

"Yes! Back there! In that trench in the field. He was trapped. He's all right now. My friend's with him."

"Jump in, miss! No, better not! The boy's father is my foreman. He's back along the lane with a van. Look, I'll get on to the trench. You ride on and tell him what's happened."

Without wasting a second more, the man let in the clutch and sent the Land-Rover leaping up the lane. Pam cycled on, a little of the urgency gone now, and fairly soon came upon the boy's father with the van. His distracted expression relaxed a little as she explained things to him. Putting the cycle into the van, she climbed into the passenger seat and they tore back up the lane.

Arriving at the trench, puffed from the run over the field, they found that Cherry was out of the trench, sitting on the grass and trying to quieten the boy, who was now crying lustily. The man Pam had first met was standing by rather helplessly. The youngster, upon seeing his father, burst into even louder tears, scrambled from Cherry and sprinted into welcoming arms.

"That proves he's okay, 'cept for shock, Frank!" the man by Cherry cried with a relieved laugh. "Take him back to his mother. I'll bring the girls along to the farm."

The father started to thank the girls, but they insisted that he hurried off home with the lad and not to worry about them.

"Well, girls," the other man said after introducing himself as Farmer Shepley, "I see how it happened. Frank missed the lad a couple of hours ago. Never thought the little imp would get this far. That trench is dangerous. The sandy soil has made the laying of the new water main a difficult job, but I never thought there'd be anyone here who didn't know about it."

"I think the little boy must have followed us," Pam said slowly. "He saw us on the lane when we fell off our cycles."

"Followed you? Up here?" the farmer queried.

"Yes!" Cherry gulped. "We've trespassed—been digging for Roman ruins over the hill there! We found them too and want to be allowed to excavate them."

"Roman ruins! First I knew I'd any! Hadn't we better take a look?"

They trudged to the top of the slope and Cherry showed him where they had dug. The farmer stared incredulously for a moment, then burst out laughing. Suddenly he checked himself and looked sadly at Cherry.

"I'm sorry! This isn't going to be funny to you, but I insist that you two spend the rest of the day as guests at the farm—to make up for the disappointment and to thank you for the rescue. And, anyway, you've got to let Frank and his wife thank you."

"We'd love that, but . . . but what have we found there?" Cherry asked.

"The concrete foundations of three air-raid shelter-like huts used by the Observer Corps during the war. They just knocked the huts down and covered up the concrete beds. The mounds are of the earth that wouldn't go back!"

It was a terrible blow, but Cherry saw the funny side of it. It seemed that archaeology, like other worthwhile jobs, was going to have its disappointments as well as joys!

GYPSY PINCUSHION

by BARBARA SMITH

To make this beautiful pin-cushion you will require the following:

1 piece of tan felt size 8 in. by 4 in., 1 triangle of red felt each side measuring 9 in., some scraps of felt in black and white, matching stranded silks, 2 small gilt curtain rings, ½ doz. gold safety-pins, some sawdust or kapok for stuffing, and a small quantity of black wool or crêpe hair.

With a pair of compasses draw a circle 3½ in. in diameter on strong brown paper.

Cut this circle out neatly and pin this paper pattern to the tan felt, cutting out two circles, one at a time.

Using brown paper again draw round a sixpence. Cut this circle out and, using it as a pattern, cut two white and two black circles for the eyes.

From the red felt cut a strip ¼ in. wide all along one side of the triangle. From this strip cut a circle ¼ in. in diameter for a mouth and a 3-in. length for a loop for hanging.

Using the illustration as a guide, pin the mouth and eyes in position on one of the tan circles. Be sure the eyes glance cutely to one side. Sew these features on firmly using stab stitch.

Now, place the two tan circles together with features outside and, beginning at top of head, over-cast the two together. When within 2 in. of starting-point stuff firmly, then complete the circle, thus closing the seam.

Next, take the red felt triangle and drape across the head, kerchief fashion, with all points meeting at one side. Pin this in position before stitching in place all the way round.

At the front edge catch down loops of crêpe hair or black wool for curls. Sew the curtain rings on firmly at ear positions and onto each of these fasten three safety-pins.

Finally insert ordinary pins to represent eyelashes, stitch the loop to the mid-back of the kerchief and your handiwork is complete.

AN UMBRELLA APRON

by KATHLEEN BINNS

IF you have some fair-sized scraps of material put away you can make a most attractive apron for the price of a packet of bias-binding. It is made in sections like an open umbrella.

Cut a paper pattern of one section making it 18 in. deep, 3 in. wide at the top and 6 in. at the bottom. It will look like a long triangle with the top cut away.

Place the paper pattern on the material, if possible with the straight of the material down the centre. Cut out six times in different colours.

Join together with a double seam, then bind all round the edge with a bright bias-binding.

The waistband can be of ribbon, or to provide a more protective top make it curved like a dutch apron. Line with Vilene to stiffen it and machine several rows of stitching over it. Ties can again be made of lengths of scrap material bound to match the apron.

If you wish to buy new material rayon taffeta makes a shiny umbrella apron. From several half-yards of material you could make six or seven aprons for a sale of work or for Xmas gifts, for the sections can be placed head to tail so as not to waste any rayon.

Allow three yards of bias-binding for the apron and another three for binding the ties.

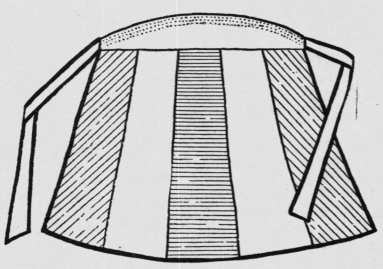

A DREAM COME TRUE

by SYLVIA ALLEN

AT the gate Rosalie kissed her mother goodbye. "Wish me luck, Mummy," she smiled, "because I've an idea I'm going to need it."

"I will keep my fingers crossed for you all day," her mother laughed. "But you'll be all right—don't worry."

So Rosalie set off to begin her first day's work as an assistant in "The Book Shop".

At last she was about to begin the job she had longed for ever since she had first visited the shop at the age of thirteen.

"It is like a dream coming true," she thought.

Yet her blue eyes clouded anxiously, and she gave a nervous tug to her trim-fitting suit as she drew nearer the shop.

As much as she loved books, she suddenly felt that she knew practically nothing about them.

"And I shall be serving people wanting every type of book under the sun," she groaned. "And I'm only on a week's trial—just one short week to prove I can do it!"

With a determined lift of her chin she then walked through the entrance of the shop and on past a department where new books and stationery were on display, towards an office at the back.

Finding Miss Forbes in the office—the lady who had engaged her—and being told she was to be assigned to the department of old books, she was very pleased. For old books had always seemed to hold a special interest for her.

After a few further explanations, Miss Forbes then left her among the maze of rooms and passages, of which every single wall was lined from top to bottom with books.

It seemed to Rosalie that she was in the largest and most overcrowded library she had ever been in. Yet the fact that she was to be in sole charge filled her with pride and a longing to become a really first-class assistant.

Miss Forbes had given her a chart showing where to find the different sections of books, so she busied herself happily straightening and sorting books until the first customers arrived.

Then she thought: "*Now* . . . this is the test!"

Yet, surprisingly, she found her dealings with the customers much easier than she had thought.

Most of the customers came only to browse. Some buying, and some not buying. Only a few asked for a certain book, and even these were patient and unhurried.

So, although the atmosphere within the book-lined walls was one of leisurely study, for Rosalie, kept busy and happy, the time flew by with a speed she had never thought possible.

At the end of the day Miss Forbes came up to her.

"You have done very well, Rosalie," she said. "I have just been telling Mr. Ward how well you have been managing, and he is very pleased."

Rosalie thanked Miss Forbes. Then, as the name was new to her, she asked who Mr. Ward was.

"He is the owner of the shop, my dear," explained Miss Forbes. "But as he has very little to do in the actual managing of the shop, you will rarely see him. He is a great art collector and just hates to be disturbed."

"I will remember that," said Rosalie.

Miss Forbes then asked if she would like to take any of the books home with her to read.

"I would love to," replied Rosalie, remembering all the books she had seen and longed to read.

So, flushed with Miss Forbes' praise of her first day's work, she hurried straight back into her own department.

Half-way towards the passage, where she thought she had seen a book of particular interest to her, she remembered she had left the chart behind.

"Never mind, I expect I shall still be able to find it," she thought, cheerfully.

Yet as she walked on through the maze of passages and rooms, her optimism began to wane. And presently she realised that without the chart there was very little hope of her ever finding the book.

Daylight was already fading and the tiers of books throwing shadows across her path, when, coming across a door which obviously led into some sort of office, she decided to make enquiries— thinking to save herself the necessity of returning for the chart.

She knocked on the door, and on being told to enter, did so. But then she drew back with surprise. For a quick glance told her that she had entered the office of Mr. Ward. Mr. Ward, who hated to be disturbed!

The room was large, and made very light by its many windows. And all round the room, on every wall, table or shelf, were the most wonderful objects of art she had ever seen.

"Well?" said a little, rather round man, peering up at her from where he stooped over a small bronze statue.

"Oh, er . . . excuse me," was all Rosalie could manage to say.

Then, to her relief, Mr. Ward smiled. "I won't bite, y'know," he said. "Come in and have a look round. You're the new young lady, aren't you?" And, without waiting for an answer, he began to show Rosalie round the treasure-filled room.

Rosalie thoroughly enjoyed looking at the collection. But of all the beautifully executed works of art she saw, most of all she liked an oil-painting—a study of a group of gaily clothed peasants.

"It is wonderful," she said, gazing at it with admiration.

Taking it from the wall, Mr. Ward explained its history to her, telling her how the painting had originally belonged to a pair, but that the artist had refused the other to be shown.

"Whether or not it was destroyed, we do not know," he went on. "But certainly it has not been seen for many, many years. This painting is valuable,

of course, but with its mate—the lost painting—ah, yes . . ." he smiled, wistfully. "If I had that, then indeed I would be the envy of art collectors all over the world."

Presently Rosalie stood upon a stool to rehang the painting for Mr. Ward. But still enthralled by the beauty of the work, she misjudged the picture rail and to her dismay the picture slipped through her fingers to fall with a clatter upon the floor.

In horror she stared down to see that the heavy gilt frame had smashed apart,

leaving the canvas crumpled, and in one corner—torn!

"I . . . I'm so sorry," she cried, stooping to pick it up.

Mr. Ward's friendly smile dispelled in anger.

"Never have I seen such carelessness," he said coldly. "How could you treat such a work so . . . so *irreverently*?"

Rosalie listened, glumly. Then, on hearing Mr. Ward's final words, her heart sank and, fumbling blindly for the door, she fled from the shop.

"Come and see me first thing in the morning," Mr. Ward had snapped.

That, of course, could mean only one thing—she was to be dismissed. *Sacked* from the job she had so quickly learned to love!

Now, instead of returning to tell her mother of how well she had fared, she would tell her of how she had ruined the pride of Mr. Ward's collection. How, in the morning, she was to be sacked. Not because she could not do the job, but through carelessness. Her dream of working in "The Book Shop" was not to come true, after all.

Never before had she spent such a miserable evening—or night. And so it was that she arrived, pale and heavy-eyed through lack of sleep, outside Mr. Ward's office the following morning.

Timidly she knocked upon the door, and this time when she entered Mr. Ward did not greet her with a smile, but nodded curtly for her to wait until he should finish reading the papers upon his desk.

She saw that the crumpled oil-painting still lay on the table where she had placed it, and noticed that the extent of the damage was not really as bad as she had thought, and could easily be repaired.

Then suddenly she moved to inspect the painting closer. For surely, underneath the torn corner of the oil-painting, she could see another layer of canvas?

Gingerly she removed the broken frame to carefully lift the painting away. And what she saw beneath it made her gasp with surprise.

The canvas was another oil-painting, which even before she looked at the signature she knew was by the same artist!

"It's the . . . the *mate*!" she cried. "The lost painting!"

Two quick strides brought Mr. Ward to her side. "The long-lost painting!" he exclaimed. "You've found it!" And he all but danced Rosalie round the room in his excitement.

"Now—*now* at last, I can tell the world that the lost painting has been found," he said, when in a calmer state. "And found by *you*!"

Then it seemed he remembered just why Rosalie was in his office.

"Yes . . . let me see, you're on a week's trial, aren't you?" he said.

"Y-yes," said Rosalie, hesitantly.

"Well, you can forget all about that—and from now on look upon yourself as being *established*."

Rosalie smiled with happiness. So she wasn't to be sacked after all!

"Oh, thank you, Mr. Ward," she said.

"If there's one thing I appreciate, it is a person who recognises a work of art when they see one," chuckled Mr. Ward.

So Rosalie returned to her work at "The Book Shop", light of heart, and confident in the security of a job she loved.

THE MAELSTROM

by W. H. MORRIS

IT was a perfect summer morning, without a cloud in the sky, as Greta Olsen and her father left their hotel and walked down to the tiny harbour at Lundenes. Lundenes is a small fishing village in Moske, which is one of the Lofoten islands. The Lofotens lie off the west coast of Norway, and Professor Olsen was studying the wild birds which make their homes there. Every day he and Greta went cruising among the smaller, uninhabited islands in a twelve-foot sailing dinghy called the *Elsa*.

This morning they headed for Gullhagen, which is little more than a mass of weather-beaten rock, where nothing grows except thin, wiry grass and a kind of lichen. Greta was steering, and she ran the dinghy into a small cove between beetling, horseshoe cliffs where it is usually possible to land in fair weather. In a rough sea it is impossible to land anywhere on Gullhagen.

Professor Olsen always liked to be alone when he was bird-watching, and now he took his binoculars and note-book, and a little ciné-camera, and made his way along the rough beach to the other end of the island. Greta settled down with a book.

It was very peaceful on Gullhagen, with no sound to break the sultry stillness save the drowsy murmur of the sea and the occasional cry of a bird.

But presently Greta heard the faint *put-put-put-put-put* of an engine, and a motor-boat rounded a headland and entered the cove.

"Oh dear!" the girl thought, puckering her smooth brow into a frown. "I do hope the sound of the engine doesn't startle the wild birds."

Greta recognised the motor-boat as the *Viking*. It belonged to an English boy named Jim Brent, who was spending a holiday in Norway, cruising up and down the famous fiords. For the last few days Jim had been staying in Lundenes, at the same hotel as the Olsens, and he and Greta had become quite friendly.

But now she felt rather angry with the English boy.

"Why does he come here with his noisy motor-boat when Father is bird-watching," she thought impatiently.

Just then the *Viking's* engine backfired, and the noise echoed and re-echoed from the tall cliffs, sending clouds of sea-birds wheeling into the air from their nesting-places with loud screams of protest.

"Bother!" thought Greta, and she was still frowning when Jim ran the little motor-boat onto the beach and jumped ashore.

"God dag!" he said, using one of the very few Norwegian phrases which he had mastered.

"Good morning," Greta replied coldly; but Jim Brent didn't appear to notice that anything was amiss.

"I say," he went on cheerfully, "I've never seen so many birds. There must be thousands of them."

And he shielded his eyes with his hands as he stared at the clouds of sea-fowl whirling above the cove.

"The noise of your motor-boat has disturbed them," Greta said. Like most young Norwegians she spoke good English. "My father was trying to take some pictures of the birds on their nests, and now it will not be possible to do so until the birds settle down again," she added sternly.

"Oh, gosh!" Jim said. "I didn't realise that. I'm awfully sorry."

He looked so abashed Greta relented a little.

"Well," she said. "I suppose you were not to know my father was bird-watching on Gullhagen."

Then they saw the professor coming along the beach towards them.

"Good morning," he said to Jim, in his polite, rather solemn way.

"Good morning, sir," Jim answered, and blushed furiously. "I say, I'm awfully sorry if I disturbed the birds."

Professor Olsen sighed inwardly, but he gave Jim a courteous smile.

"You were not to know I was bird-watching," he answered; and Jim felt more guilty than ever.

"I'm constantly having trouble with that engine," he said lamely. "I'll have it thoroughly over-hauled when I get back to Bergen."

"It might be well to do so," Professor Olsen said mildly. "It can be dangerous cruising off these coasts with a faulty motor."

After that there was an awkward silence.

"Well, sir, I'm awfully sorry about

this," the boy said at last, in a confused voice. "I'll clear off at once so as not to disturb the birds again."

"Takk, thank you," the professor said politely; and Jim pushed off from the beach, and went *put-putting* away out of the cove.

"I suppose the English boy has spoilt everything with his noisy old motor-boat," Greta said; and her father nodded.

"I'm afraid he has, my dear," he answered. "It will be useless trying to photograph the birds until they settle down again, so we may as well spend the time having our mid-dag."

"Beastly noisy thing!" Greta said—meaning the *Viking*.

And they settled down to eat the sandwiches and drink the milk which they had brought with them for their midday meal.

The following day Professor Olsen found that he had run out of film for his camera, so Greta offered to run across to the mainland for a fresh supply whilst her father was busy getting his notes in order.

There was a hint of mist in the sunshine as she left the hotel, and Greta looked at the brassy sky and wondered if there was a storm brewing. However, the prospect didn't alarm her, because she was used to sailing the *Elsa* in all sorts of weather.

Jim Brent came hurrying down to the little wooden jetty as Greta was casting off.

"Hallo! God morgen," he said rather doubtfully, because he wasn't quite sure what his reception was going to be after what had happened the previous day.

But Greta had quite forgiven him.

"Good morning," she answered with a sunny smile.

Jim perked up when he saw that he was forgiven.

"I say, if you want to cross to the mainland I'll take you in my motor-boat," he said eagerly. "It will be a lot quicker."

Greta smiled again, and shook her head.

"Takk! Thanks!" she answered. "But I prefer sailing in the *Elsa*. There is no fun with a motor-boat—a sailing dinghy is much better. You need skill to handle a sail."

Jim looked rather crestfallen.

"Maybe," he said. "But a motor-boat is a lot more reliable. You don't have to depend on the wind."

Greta smiled and changed the subject.

"Where are you going today?" she asked.

Jim waved vaguely towards the south.

"I was thinking of running down to Vaeroy," he replied.

Greta stopped smiling then, and looked rather serious.

"I do not think you should cross the Strom Channel today," she said in her rather precise English. "There is a strong tide running, and there may be a maelstrom if the wind rises."

"I say! Do you really think so?" Jim cried eagerly. "I've been hoping I might see the famous maelstrom whilst I was here. Is it true that it can wreck even a large sailing vessel?"

"Such stories are very exaggerated," Greta answered gravely. "But it is dangerous to cross the Strom Channel in a small boat at the time of the mael-

strom. Many people have been drowned there. You must keep away from it."

"But I should love to see the maelstrom," Jim said. "That really *would* be something to talk about when I get back to England."

And he grinned with excitement.

"Please, it is better you do not go near the maelstrom if you see it forming," Greta told him earnestly. "It would be better, I think, if you did not cross the Strom Channel today."

"Oh, but I shall be all right in a motor-boat," Jim answered. "But don't worry—I'll keep well clear of the maelstrom if there is one."

Secretly he thought that Greta was being a little silly and exaggerating the danger.

"Well, please be careful," the girl said, and pushed off from the jetty where the *Elsa* had been tied up.

"Adjo!" Jim called after her; using another of his slender stock of Norwegian words.

"Adjo! Goodbye," Greta replied with a smile and a friendly wave of her hand.

Jim stood for a few minutes watching the *Elsa* as the little sailing dinghy went skimming across the water.

"Greta certainly knows how to handle a sailing-boat," he thought. "But I can't understand her preferring a sailing-boat to a motor-boat."

And, shaking a puzzled head, Jim made his way to where the *Viking* was moored.

Starting up the motor, he went chugging out of the tiny harbour, and headed south for the Strom Channel which separates Moske and the main group of islands from Vaeroy and a cluster of tiny islets at the southern-most tip of the Lofotens.

Jim made a landing on Vaeroy, and ate the picnic lunch which he had brought with him. Afterwards he explored the island, although there was little to be seen except great masses of weathered rock which looked as old as time itself. Finally, early in the afternoon he left Vaeroy, and headed back across the Strom Channel for Moske.

The wind was rising, and copper-coloured clouds were piling up above the western horizon, but Jim didn't worry because he expected to be back in Lundenes long before the threatened storm could break.

Presently, however, the steady *put-put-put* of the motor broke into a stutter, and finally ceased altogether. Jim worked the throttle, and the engine coughed and spluttered several times, but then went dead again.

"Bother!" Jim muttered, and spent some time trying to discover the cause of the breakdown.

By this time the wind had veered to the east, and the sea had the oily smoothness which is usual during the fifteen minutes "slack" at the turn of the tide. But Jim still didn't realise that he was in any danger, and he was more irritated than alarmed by the failure of the engine.

"I ought to have had it overhauled before I left Bergen," he thought regretfully.

But presently he looked up from fiddling with the motor, and was startled to see several enormous streaks of foam on the surface of the water. As he watched, these streaks grew steadily bigger, and spread rapidly in all directions, until they formed a number of whirlpools, which went spinning like great wheels of polished steel.

"It must be the maelstrom," Jim thought; and for the first time he felt a sudden chill of fear.

"I had better get clear of this," he thought, remembering Greta's warning, and, getting out the oars, he started to row.

But he seemed to make little or no progress; and meanwhile the separate whirlpools spread, and joined together, until they formed one vast, spinning circle of water, a mile or more in diameter. There was an outer belt of surf, which revolved around an inner circle of inky-black water, and this central vortex was shaped like a gigantic funnel, with sides which slanted at a steepish angle to the horizon. As it revolved the giant whirlpool gave out a deep, continuous roar like thunder.

Jim rowed desperately in an effort to get clear of the maelstrom, but all his efforts were in vain. Before long the crippled motor-boat was drawn into the outer rim of broken water, where it heeled over so alarmingly Jim thought it was going to capsize.

In a moment of panic he lost one of his oars; and although the *Viking* righted herself, Jim found it quite hopeless to try to manœuvre her with a single oar.

Presently she was swept into the central portion of the maelstrom, and carried round and round by the whirlpool, each revolution bringing her nearer and nearer to the bottomless black gulf at the centre of the vortex. Jim could see odds-and-ends of flotsam spinning wildly around there, until finally they were sucked down into the watery maw like matchsticks carried down a drain-pipe.

It was quite useless now to row with only one oar, and all that Jim could do was to cling desperately to the sides of the boat, as it went spinning nearer and nearer to the rumbling centre of the vortex.

Whilst Jim was exploring Vaeroy, Greta had made her trip to the mainland, and bought the films her father needed, and done some other shopping. Then she set off to sail back across the Vest Fiord, to Lundenes. With a strong wind filling the *Elsa*'s sail, the little vessel seemed to skim the top of the waves like a sea-swallow.

The wind was rising steadily, and soon long, white-tipped, hissing rollers were running before it in endless succession. At one moment the *Elsa* would hang poised on the crest of a wave: the next she would go plunging giddily down into a deep, wide trough of ice-green water as though she never would climb clear again.

Most people would have found it rather alarming, but Greta loved the sea when it was like this. She liked the cold tingle of flying spray against her cheeks, and the feel of the wind ruffling her hair; and she handled the tiny vessel with a skill that none of the fishermen of Lundenes could have bettered.

Presently she became aware of a far-off rumble like thunder; but although the storm-clouds were black and threatening above the western horizon, Greta knew that it was not thunder she heard.

Thunder did not rumble continuously like this. Then, as the *Elsa* struggled to the crest of the next wave, Greta saw, far away down the Strom Channel, the vast circle of foam which was the outer rim of the maelstrom.

But she saw something else—something which made her gasp with dismay. It was the *Viking* being carried round in the grip of the giant whirlpool.

Greta was both puzzled and alarmed. The English boy seemed to be making no effort to get clear of the maelstrom. Was he deliberately letting the *Viking* be sucked towards the centre of the vortex, not understanding how dangerous it was? Greta did not realise that the motor-boat's engine was silent, for the roar of the giant whirlpool swallowed all lesser sounds.

"I must warn the English boy. He does not know the danger," Greta thought anxiously. "Even a motor-boat will be capsized and wrecked if it gets too near to the heart of the maelstrom."

And she put the tiller hard over, so that the *Elsa* came round in a flurry of flying spray, and headed down the Strom Channel, straight for the maelstrom.

As she neared the outer rim of surf Greta waved and called to Jim, although she knew that her words would be drowned by the thunderous rumble of the maelstrom. She saw the boy wave and call back, and she beckoned to him to get clear of the deadly whirlpool.

And then, in dumb show, Jim made her realise that the *Viking*'s engine had failed. Greta felt suddenly numb with horror as she realised the full extent of his peril.

She looked about her desperately, but there was no other vessel in sight, and there was no time (she knew) to get to

Lundenes and send a motor-boat to the rescue. Unless *she* could save him, the English boy was doomed.

Greta knew how easily her little sailing dinghy could come to grief in the maelstrom, and for a moment her heart misgave her. But then she forgot her own fear as she saw Jim's pale, terrified face staring at her across the waste of water.

"I *must* save him," she thought. And, with a quick glance at the bellying sail, she eased the tiller over, and the *Elsa* sailed into the outer ring of surf.

Here the seas had neither shape nor regular movement, but charged and buffeted one another in a crazy dance, and flung great spouts of ice-green water into the air.

Greta was drenched with clouds of flying spray, and nearly deafened by the angry clamour of the waves; but she was too busy now handling tiller and sail to

be afraid any longer. For some seconds that seemed never-ending the little vessel pitched and tossed alarmingly, and only Greta's clever seamanship saved the *Elsa* from being swamped or capsized.

The dinghy shuddered like a living thing, and an almost solid wall of water nearly swept Greta over the side. But then, suddenly—miraculously, it seemed —they were clear of that welter of angry, tormented waves and in the smooth-spinning inner circle of the maelstrom.

The *Elsa* righted herself, and, with the wind filling her sail, she rapidly overhauled the derelict *Viking*. Words were useless because the dread rumble of the maelstrom filled the air and stifled all other sounds. But as the space between the two vessels narrowed, Greta motioned to Jim to jump.

He nodded to show that he understood, and Greta saw him rise cautiously

to his feet. Then as he crouched, half standing, half kneeling in the *Viking*'s stern, gripping the gunwales with both hands, she steered the *Elsa* as close as she dared.

"Jump!" she screamed; and although her words were lost in the thunderous din of the maelstrom, Jim understood. He took a desperate leap, and half fell into the *Elsa*'s bows, and the dinghy reeled alarmingly.

But once again she righted herself, and Greta steered for the outer circle of the maelstrom.

Now, however, they were being sucked back down the long, gleaming slope of the vortex. Sick with despair and dread, they found themselves looking down into the black, bottomless gulf at the heart of the vortex.

And then, just in the nick of time, a violent bluster of wind came screaming down out of the sky, and the *Elsa*'s sail whipped and bulged as though it would be torn clean from the masthead. The dinghy heeled over, and for a moment they thought she was going to turn turtle.

But then she seemed to shake herself, and she leapt forward, her slim bows cleaving the glassy-smooth water of the vortex as she drove before the wind. Straight for the outer ring of the maelstrom she ran; and once again Greta needed all her skill to keep the dinghy from foundering amid the welter of leaping waves.

But at last they escaped into the comparatively smooth water beyond, and the danger was past.

"You saved my life," Jim said shakily, as soon as they could hear themselves speak. "I don't know how I can ever thank you."

Greta tossed the wet hair out of her eyes, as she clung to the tiller with both hands.

"Please," she said in her quiet, practical way. "There is no time to talk—you must bale. We have shipped much water."

But she gave him a quick, friendly smile.

MAKE YOUR OWN CROSSWORD PUZZLES

by
ROBERT REEVES

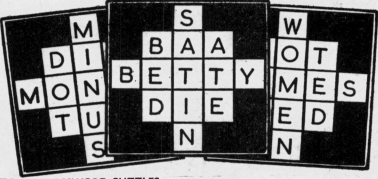

FIG. I. CROSSWORD PUZZLES

FIG. 2. SYMMETRICAL PATTERNS

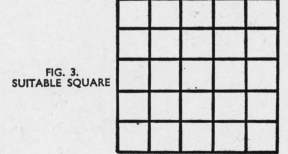

FIG. 3.
SUITABLE SQUARE

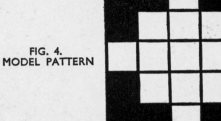

FIG. 4.
MODEL PATTERN

IT is easy to make original crossword puzzles (Fig. 1), if you observe the following instructions:

1. Make the form of the puzzle symmetrical (viz.: if one corner is blackened out, the other three should be also) (Fig. 2).

2. Use short words rather than long ones. (Until you become proficient, five squares to a line, vertically and horizontally, are sufficient (Fig. 3). You can reduce the number of squares on a line by blackening out the corners (Fig. 2).

3. Begin with a simple pattern. You will be able to make numerous puzzles if you fit your words into the model pattern shown in Fig. 4.

4. Number the vertical and horizontal lines as indicated in Fig. 5.

FIG. 5. LINE NUMBERS

FIG. 6. FIRST WORD

FIG. 7. SECOND WORD

5. Fill in the longest vertical line with a word of five letters, but be careful to select a word that has a vowel for all its even letters. (Let us assume the word you have chosen is "DORIS"—see Fig. 6. Note the position of the vowels.)

6. Choose another word of five letters to fit across the centre. (As we are using the word "DORIS", in this case the middle letter must be "R".) Refer Fig. 7.

7. Now select a third word, but remember the last letter will form the beginning of another word (Fig. 8).

8. The fourth word is now to be completed (Fig. 9).

9. Lastly, insert a letter that will begin line 5 across, and end line 3 down (Fig. 10).

10. All that now remains to be done is to provide clues that will enable competitors to guess the words you have chosen.

For the selected words in the diagrams you could use the following descriptions:

Down
1. A girl's name.
3. A suggestion.
4. Plural of "Man".

Across
2. Engaged labour.
3. A boy's name.
5. A pointed fastener.

If you have any difficulty in describing a word, turn it up in a dictionary and use the description given.

FIG. 8. THIRD WORD

FIG. 9. FOURTH WORD

FIG. 10. FIFTH WORD

UNCLE OSTRICH

by WINIFRED NORLING

"IT really is too bad of our parents to foist us on Uncle Oliver at a moment's notice like this," declared Vanda Wingrove. "It's not done. Why, the poor man couldn't refuse to have us, no matter how much he wanted to. There just wasn't time."

"Oh, I don't know," her sister Karin said thoughtfully. "He could have wired us to go to Aunt Anna."

"Not if he's human," Vanda laughed. "Aunt Anna's the absolute end. *You* know it, and *he* must know it."

"I think he'll like having us," said Karin. "It's up to us to make him, anyway. Actually, it should be rather fun, Van. I know you're not as keen on writing as I am, but you've a nose for news, and that's invaluable to anyone working on a newspaper."

"But we're not working on a newspaper," Vanda expostulated, her brown eyes wide.

"We soon shall be if I've any say in the matter," chuckled her sister. "It's just the chance I've been waiting for, and I can't pretend I'm sorry we're on our way to Riverborne."

"You always were a jolly little optimist, Kar. You know Mother's always told us that Uncle hates interfering females. That's why we've never spent any of our holidays with him. I quite expect the newspaper office will be forbidden ground."

"He's a bachelor, isn't he?" questioned Karin thoughtfully.

Vanda nodded.

"Good. Then you've a fine chance to win him. You *can* cook, if it's the only thing you do excel in, and he's probably putting up with an inefficient housekeeper. You can stay at home and cook luscious meals, while I go to the office and make a niche for myself on Uncle's paper. Do you know what it's called?"

"The *Riverborne Gazette*, I think. Don't you remember that friend of Mummy's sent her a copy when her daughter was married. The friend's, I mean, of course."

"I remember now. If I have my way, I'll be a cub reporter before the end of the week. I've reread that career book on becoming a journalist Molly gave me, so I know all the gen."

For a moment Vanda stared at her sister in astonishment, then she began to laugh.

"I can see you've got it all taped. I

only hope Uncle Oliver thinks as you do, or I can foresee fireworks. I don't mind taking on the cooking, but I seem to remember Mother saying Uncle had a wonderful housekeeper. I think she was their nurse years ago, so she'll be old and probably set in her ways."

"Well, if the worst comes to the worst, you'll have to be a cub reporter, too," Karin said airily. "I wonder if our dear uncle will meet us at the station. Do you think you'll know him, Van?"

"Of course I shan't, unless he's terribly like Mummy. I've only seen him once, when I was about two. I remember you howled all the time. I daresay that's why he never came again. You *were* a noisy baby!"

"And you weren't, I suppose. I'm not worrying about being met. If we're not claimed, we'll just take a taxi."

There was nobody at Riverborne Station at all likely to be Oliver Rich, and, after waiting a few minutes, the girls were just about to leave, when a young man approached them.

"Are you by any chance Mr. Rich's nieces?" he asked, with a friendly grin.

"We certainly are, and it was clever of you to know it," said Karin, smiling. "I suppose our uncle asked you to meet us. That was thoughtful of him."

The young man hesitated, and did not answer for a moment.

"Well, actually, he didn't," he admitted. "Of course he would have if he'd thought of it, but he's terribly worried. Half the staff are away with flu, and now his housekeeper has had a fall and is in hospital."

"Couldn't be better——" began Karin; then she broke off, flushing.

"That sounds pretty awful of me, but, you see, we want Uncle Oliver to like having us, and my sister Vanda's a wonderful cook. She'll run the house beautifully, and I can help out on the paper. I want to be a journalist more than anything in the world, but my parents aren't a scrap enthusiastic. If I can get Uncle on my side, they'll give in and let me train."

The young man laughed.

"I felt like that once, but a newspaper-man's life's not a bed of roses, you know, not unless they're ones with long thorny stems. My name's Andrew Paterson, but everyone calls me Andy. I knew you were expected today, and as I had to be in this part of the world, I thought I'd welcome you to Riverborne."

"Jolly nice of you, Andy," said Vanda warmly. "Where do we go from here?"

For a moment Andy stood frowning thoughtfully.

"There won't be anyone at the house, and I haven't a key, so you'd better come straight to the office. The Big Man'll be there, and he can either give you a key, run you home himself, or let you stay at the office till he's ready to go. I must get back and write up my stuff, anyway, so come along."

As they entered the offices of the *Riverborne Gazette* both girls felt thrilled and excited. Karin took a deep breath as they mounted the stairs, and breathed in the fascinating smell of printer's ink, and listened to the dull rumbling sound that came from far below. When they reached the door with O. S. T. Rich on it, Andy asked them to wait. He knocked and disappeared inside. Karin turned to Vanda.

"Look!" she whispered. "I'd never thought of it before. I suppose I didn't know all his initials. I shall call him Uncle Ostrich in future. I wonder if that's his nickname here. I must ask Andy."

"Ssh!" warned Vanda. "Someone's coming."

It was only Andy, and he beckoned to them.

"He's in there. Go right in. He's waiting for you. I must fly."

A moment later the sisters found themselves in their uncle's inner office, and he rose to greet them.

"Sorry I could not meet you," he apologised, "but we're terribly short-staffed, thanks to this flu epidemic. 'Twas a good thing Andy remembered. I'm afraid I can't run you home yet, and there's no one there to let you in. Could you hang about here, or get something to eat in the town? I'll be free about six."

"That's all right, Uncle. Don't worry about us. Perhaps I can help. I can type, you know, and I hope to be a journalist one day. If you've a spare key, Vanda could go and get an evening meal ready. She's a jolly good cook, and I'm sure you'll be wanting something hot after a day's hard work."

Oliver Rich smiled.

"I did not expect two such capable nieces," he told them. "I suppose I thought of you still as little girls. I know I said something to Mrs. Hudson about not having any toys."

"I'm sixteen, Uncle, and want to leave school at the end of the summer term. Vanda's a year older, so she's leaving then, in any case, and going to a domestic college to acquire the cordon bleu touch. I'd rather eat than make the things. I think it's a queer choice, and I only hope she's not making a mistake, because she has a nose for news."

"Has she indeed! But being able to cook is always an asset, my dear. So you want to be a journalist. We must talk about it some time. I can't stop now. We won't worry about a cooked meal at home tonight. We'll dine out to celebrate your arrival. Now run along and let me get on with my work. Go along the passage to the door marked REPORTERS. You may be able to help Howard, my chief reporter. He's nearly desperate for lack of staff. Good-bye for now, and I hope you'll be very happy in Riverborne."

"He's a poppet," breathed Vanda, as they stole along the passage. "But you were quite right, Kar. He looks as though he wants feeding up. One of the buttons on his coat's loose, too."

Karin giggled, but before she could answer, they reached the reporters' room and went in. Singling out an older man sitting at the largest desk in the room, Karin went up to him.

"Are you Mr. Howard?" she asked.

"I am, and you'll be the Big Man's nieces. Welcome to Riverborne. How can I help you?"

"By giving us a job," Karin told him. "Uncle says you're desperate for reporters, so can you use us? We're normally intelligent, and can carry out orders. I can type, too. Not top-speed, of course, but fairly accurate."

Jim Howard grinned, and, leaning forward, dragged a big book towards him.

"Half today's entries haven't been covered," he sighed. "Andy can't be everywhere, and the other three are down with flu. Not feeling too good myself actually, or I'd be out on the job. Still, someone's got to be here in case something breaks unexpectedly. Can't leave the phone in the copy-boys' hands. Do you think you could handle a bazaar? Our parish church—St. Peter's—is having one this afternoon. You'll be too late for the opening, of course, but you could get the low-down from some of the stall-holders. Get a list of the stalls, and be careful to have the names of those in charge of them absolutely accurate. We'll only need a short piece of description and general interest, but we ought to have that, and it's risky to do it without going and seeing what's on. Think you can manage that?"

"Of course. Where is the bazaar? At the Church Hall?" asked Karin.

"Yes. Turn left outside the entrance, and take the second turning to your left. Here are note-books and pencils, and you'll need passes. Good. Be as quick as you can, and good hunting."

Karin took the cards, and handed one to her sister. Soon the two girls were hurrying along the street.

"Isn't this fun!" gurgled Karin. "When you got up this morning you never expected to be a press representative before the day was out."

"We shouldn't be now if it weren't for the flu epidemic," Vanda reminded her.

"The cause doesn't matter if only we make a success of it," declared Karin quickly. "Here we are. The charmingly beflagged building welcomed all who came to swell the funds at St. Peter's

bazaar this afternoon," she began. Then she giggled. "Come on, Van. Show your pass as though you're used to it. No one must guess we're new to the job."

"What do we do now?" asked Vanda, when they were safely inside.

"Find the organiser, or someone in authority, and get the gen," Karin whispered back. "I'll do that, if you like, while you go round and make notes about the stalls. It's obviously an Elizabethan setting, and you can describe the dresses too, if you like."

At first Mrs. Grahame-Lowe was not at all friendly. She was annoyed that the *Gazette* had not had someone

present to cover the opening ceremony, but when she heard about the influenza epidemic, and how Mr. Rich had sent his own nieces to give her bazaar a good write-up, she unbent. Soon the sisters had all the necessary information, and, after checking it, they returned to the office, and Karin wrote up what she considered was a good account. But when she wanted to give it to Mr. Howard, he was nowhere to be found. While she was wondering what to do, Andy came in.

"Hello, you two. Gosh, I'm tired! Who'd be a news-man? It's nothing but disappointments and bunions."

Karin laughed.

"Where's Mr. Howard?" she asked. "We've done the bazaar, and I want to give him the copy."

"'Fraid you won't be able to. He's had to give in and go home. Everything's to go to the Big Man himself. Shall I cast my eye over it for you first?"

"Please. If I've made a mess of it, I'd rather he didn't know."

"Not at all bad," commented Andy, when he had scanned the account. "But too long, I'm afraid. You'll need to cut out about a third of the flowery part, and then it'll be ready for the compositors. Cutting is really the sub-editors' job, but there's only one of 'em left, poor bloke, and he's asleep on his feet. Look, shall I blue-pencil it? Then you can retype it and take it along to your uncle."

"O.K." Karin did not sound enthusiastic, but she realised that Andy knew more than she did about the paper's requirements. "Can you do it right away, Andy?"

"If you like. It won't take a minute."

Ten minutes later Karin was knocking on what she privately dubbed the Ostrich door.

"What do you want, Karin?" asked her uncle, frowning. "I am very busy. Jim Howard's ill now, and I must get his work done as well as my own."

"I know. I've only brought you the account of the St. Peter's bazaar. Mr. Howard sent us to cover it. Would you like us to do anything else? If this is all right, of course."

Without a word Oliver Rich took the shortened version and scanned it.

"Not bad," he admitted. "'Twill have to do, anyway. I only hope you've got all the names correctly. These wretched females are so touchy. There's nothing more now, but there'll be plenty to-morrow. Andy must cover the magistrates' courts, so he'll be glad of you two for other things. He'll tell you what to do."

"Thanks, Uncle Ostrich!" exclaimed

Karin, her eyes shining. "We'll not let you down."

A momentary smile touched the lips of the editor, but all he said was: "Fix things with Andy, but remember, my paper means everything to me. No matter what it costs you, never let down the *Riverborne Gazette*."

"I won't," Karin promised, and she hurried off to tell Vanda what their uncle had said.

For the next few days things in the newspaper office were more than hectic. The sisters helped Andy as much as they could, and Karin was in her element. Then, on the very day two compositors and a sub-editor returned to the office, Oliver Rich succumbed to the virus, and had to stay in bed. Vanda looked worried.

"I must stay at home, Karin," she declared. "If I don't, Uncle's sure to do something mad, and Dr. Horden says he *must* be kept warm in bed for at least two or three days."

"Of course you must be here," Karin agreed. "More of the staff are gradually creeping back, so we'll cope. I'll get there early and fix things with Andy. Mr. Howard is expected back in a day or two, and I'm becoming quite expert at being in six places at once. You keep Uncle happy, and you'll be doing a worthwhile job."

Although Karin arrived at the office early, Andy was already on the job.

"Oh, good! I'm glad you've come," he greeted her. "I ought to be going, or I'll be late for the Agricultural Show. It starts today, and I shall have to be there all the morning. I've made a list for you, and whatever you don't do, cover the items I've starred. They're of first importance. I know I can rely on you. Fortunately Mr. Byrne is back this morning. He's the news editor, so if I'm still out when you return, go to him."

"Good thing he's back," Karin said with feeling. "Uncle's gone down now, and the doctor insists on at least three days in bed."

"Good gods and goddesses!" cried Andy. "That's just about the end. Well, we can only do our best. You'd better go and break it to David Byrne. He'll have to make the decisions and act the Big Man. Thank goodness he's back! I must fly. So long, and remember the stars."

Andy was halfway down the stairs before Karin could answer, so she just shrugged her shoulders and went to find Mr. Byrne. In spite of herself, she had to laugh at the look of horror that dawned in his eyes when he heard he would have to wear the Big Man's boots.

"It *would* happen to me," he groaned, "and not even Jim Howard to help out."

Half laughing, Karin fled back to the reporters' room and began to study her list. The morning slipped by, and she felt a sense of achievement at having covered both the important items when lunchtime drew near. As she was a long way from the office, she decided to have a snack meal at a coffee-bar before going to the station to meet a famous actress at just after twelve o'clock. She reached the station with a few minutes to spare, and then suddenly realised with dismay that she did not know from which town

the actress was coming. How could she find out at which platform to wait?

"Surely if she's famous she'll be coming from London," she reasoned. "I'd better find out when the next train from London is due."

There was one at the given time, and so Karin hopefully made her way to Platform 3. But when the train arrived, no one resembling a famous actress alighted. Worried, Karin hurried to the ticket barrier and waited. If only Andy had written the actress's full name! Karin supposed she ought to know to whom the B.M. referred, but she just could not think of anyone with those initials.

Suddenly she noticed a small group of people coming towards the exit, followed by two porters with a great deal of luggage. She heard one of the young men address a pretty girl as Betty, and she decided to act. As they came through the barrier, she approached them, saying, "I am from the *Riverborne Gazette*, and I should like to ask you a few questions, if I may."

The pretty girl beamed.

"Dennis," she called, "it's the Press. They want a notice for the local rag."

"Jolly civil of them," declared the tall grey-haired man who had been talking to the porters. "Tell your readers, young lady, that we are happy to be in Riverborne, and that Miss Betty Marsden will love playing for them. I'll send along particulars of our plays to your newspaper, with the names of the actors, and I thank you for your courtesy in welcoming us. We all appreciate your goodwill, but I'm afraid we can't stay longer now as we must rehearse. Good afternoon. By the way, which is your paper?"

"The *Riverborne Gazette*," murmured Karin, with an awful feeling that something was very wrong. Famous actresses weren't grateful to newspapers for meeting them. Puzzled, she stood watching the laughing group leave the station, and then she recklessly hailed a taxi and sped back to the office. If only Andy were back! He was, and he looked up from his machine as she burst into the room.

"Where's the fire?" he demanded. "And what in heaven's name are you doing here?" he went on, glancing at his watch. "Surely you ought to be out at the airport gathering up the crumbs of caviar that fall from the great Merle Bancroft's sandwiches."

"The — the airport!" stammered Karin, her face white. "Merle B-Ban-

croft. I don't understand. At least, I think I'm beginning to. Oh, Andy! Why couldn't you have been more explicit?"

"More explicit!" burst out the indignant reporter. "I like that. Surely the whole town knows Merle Bancroft's coming here today for a special charity matinée."

"I didn't," Karin almost sobbed. "I haven't had time to *read* the newspapers recently, and no one's mentioned it to me. I haven't been to the airport—I didn't even know there was one so near. I went to the station and met an actress called Betty Marsden. She and her party seemed delighted to see me, and they'll

be sending along all the gen for us. I'll own I was puzzled by their ready co-operation. That's why I dashed back here to check. What on earth can I do?"

For a moment Andy frowned; then he began to laugh.

"That's what comes of roping in tiros," he said. "I'll ring up George of the *Echo*. If I can make him see the joke, he might help out, though I doubt it. You've done your job so well, I forget you're new to it and don't know Riverborne and what's happening here. Evidently you met the repertory company that's arrived for the season. Well, it's good to be on friendly terms with them. It may

bear fruit later. We must put in something about Merle B. or the Big Man will blow his top. It's considered a feather in Riverborne's cap that Merle Bancroft was persuaded to give this matinée here. Can't really think why she did. Don't look so blue, Kar. It's more my fault than yours. Good thing your uncle's in bed. That gives me a chance to bring home at least a rasher of the pig."

But, try as he would, Andy could get no details of the great arrival, and the *Riverborne Gazette* were only able to print a short non-committal paragraph. Fortunately, Merle Bancroft had refused to talk to reporters, so not even the *Echo* had much to tell.

Vanda was very understanding when Karin arrived home after seven and told her what had happened.

"How were you to know?" she insisted. "It was Andy's fault. Uncle's better, anyway, and so is Mrs. Hudson. I slipped into the hospital to enquire when I was out shopping, and they let me see her. She expects to be home in a week."

"Good. I say, Van, will Uncle be well enough to be left for a bit to-morrow? I'd like you to come with me to see the Easter Carnival Trades procession. I've to write it up, and I've lost my nerve. I'm terrified I'll miss something important. Andy says I'm only fit for safe jobs like fires and funerals."

"Of course I'll come if you want me. Mrs. Hudson says Mrs. Fowler across the road will come in if I want to go out or need help."

"Good. David Byrne's going to watch from the office windows—he has to be there for the phone—so he'll write up the description of the floats and the actual procession. He wants me to mingle with the crowd and try to get their personal reactions. Public opinion matters a lot in a job like ours."

Early the following afternoon the sisters set off to find a place where they could see the procession, and where there were plenty of people. But early as they were, hundreds of people were earlier.

"We can't fight our way through this," panted Vanda, clutching her handbag tightly. "Can't we use our press passes to get through?"

"Course not. The whole point in finding out what people think of this year's do is to let them think we're just ordinary sightseers. Breathe the word Press, and they're immediately suspicious and shut up like clams. Let's cut down this side turning, and get back on to the route farther along. We might stand a better chance there."

"Doesn't seem much better," sighed Vanda, as they rejoined the crowds farther up the hill. "I say, Kar, look at that poor old soul! She'll faint in a minute if someone doesn't rescue her from the squash. You carry on with your job. I'm going to see what I can do to help her. I'll use my pass if I must."

Karin nodded and Vanda began squirming her way towards the white-faced stranger who seemed too dazed to move.

"Hold hard, missie," shouted one red-faced man. "You can't get to the front that way. You must take your chance like the rest of us. We was here first."

"I don't want your place," retorted Vanda with spirit. "My—my friend's ill, and I want to get her out of the crowd before she faints."

"That's different. Make way for the little 'un, chaps. She's not stopping. Her friend's ill."

Somehow Vanda reached the trembling woman and, slipping her arm round her, began to lead her away from the excited, pressing throng. Thanking the red-faced man, who was now helping her as much as he could, she steered the half-fainting old lady towards a nearby park that was almost deserted.

"Let's go in there where it's quiet and sit down," she suggested. "You'll soon feel better."

"You are very kind, but I'd rather go home. It's not far, and my bairnie will be worrying about me. I've been shopping, and I quite forgot the procession. I was carried along with the crowd, and couldn't get away. I'm better now."

"Then let me take you home," begged Vanda. "I hate crowds, too, and I'd feel happier if I went with you."

It was not ten minutes' walk to the neat little house where her new friend lived. As they turned in at the gate, Vanda saw an anxious face looking out of the window. Before they reached the door it was flung open by a beautiful girl in old slacks and a cream sweater.

"What's happened, Nankie?" she cried. "Are you ill?"

"She's better now. There's a terrible squash in the High Street, and your friend got caught up in it. I managed to get her away, and I thought I'd better see her home. It's the annual procession, you see, and everybody's out."

"How kind of you! Won't you come in? I'm sure you could do with a drink. You look jolly hot."

"Of course she's coming in," said the old lady firmly. "Put on the kettle, Merle dear."

As Vanda followed them into the house, her brain was reeling under the shock. She suddenly realised that the pretty girl who was putting on the kettle for her—Vanda's—tea was none other than the famous actress Merle Bancroft. But what was she doing in this little house? Vanda's nose for news was beginning to sniff. If only she could get this story, and permission to use it, Karin would make good her recent blunder. It would be a wonderful coup with which to welcome Uncle Oliver back to the office on Monday. Vanda decided to tell her new friends the whole story. She could be very amusing when she liked, and she made her listeners laugh with her account of Karin meeting the repertory company instead of Merle. When she had finished talking, there was a moment's silence. It was Nankie who broke it.

"Well, Merle, what are you going to do? Make the girl's career or ruin it?"

"I'll give you a story on one condition, Vanda."

"And that is?"

"This address must not be given. I can't have poor Nankie pestered by newshounds and photographers. Do you agree?"

"Of course. Actually, I don't know the address," Vanda laughed.

"Then I suggest you tell your readers what a simple home-loving girl Merle Bancroft is when off duty. You can tell them that you had tea with her when she was spending a weekend in Riverborne with her beloved old nurse, and that my greatest joys are cleaning windows and polishing beautiful old wood. My favourite clothes are these old slacks and any kind of comfortable sweater. I loathe winkle-pickers, and easy casuals are a must. I can't cook a thing, though I can just make a cup of tea. I have no parents, and Nankie's my world, though she does still try to rule me with a rod of iron. I usually get up at six and go for a long walk while my fans are sleeping,

and apart from Nankie I have only one love—the THEATRE. I don't want to make films, and I only appear on television when I must, but I adore the smell of grease paint and everything connected with the live theatre. Will that do?"

"Rather!" exclaimed Vanda, almost breathless with delight. "I think I've got it all down. Would you read and sign it, please, or they'll never believe it's genuine at the office."

Laughingly Merle complied, after adding a few more intimate touches, and when Vanda left the house an hour later she was walking on air. In her notebook she had the story for which the world was waiting. So little was known about Merle Bancroft's private life, that every paper, even the big London ones,

would give anything for what she, Vanda Wingrove, had. Karin must write it up and give it to Uncle Oliver, and then he would be certain to back her in her choice of a career. Though Vanda had actually got the story, she unselfishly wanted her sister to have all the honour and glory.

At first Karin would not believe her sister, and when she was at last convinced that the story was genuine, she flatly refused to use it as her own. After much persuasion, she agreed to write it up and give it in as their joint effort, but further than that she would not go.

To say that Oliver Rich and the whole newspaper staff were thrilled with the girls' effort was to put it mildly. Andy literally danced a highland fling in the reporters' room, and David Byrne was thankful to hand over the reins of office to the Big Man when he was in such high good humour.

Oozing geniality, Oliver Rich said to his nieces: "I'll take you both on and train you."

"Karin will be thrilled," Vanda told him, "but I don't think I want to be a journalist, Uncle. I'm happier with my pots and pans in the kitchen."

"You'll come to me, Karin, if your parents agree?"

"Need you ask, Uncle Ostrich? I'm afraid I'll have to stay at school till July, but when I break up I'll take the first train to Riverborne. I wish I could hug Merle Bancroft, and I will hug you, Uncle dear, for giving me my heart's desire. I can hardly realise I'm not dreaming. Thanks to you, darling Uncle Ostrich, I'm going to be a journalist, a journalist, a journalist; I'm going to be a journalist on the staff of the grand R.G."

A HANDBAG COMPENDIUM

by KATHLEEN BINNS

DON'T you find your handbag gets full of clutter? Everything gets lost and jumbled up. You wish— if only all your belongings were neatly together, all in a piece, how much simpler life would be! Well, here is an attempt to do so. At least a few things are combined—notecase and purse, rainhood, diary and pencil, comb and nail file. Not bad to get even those under one roof, is it?

You will need a 12 in. square of felt, or several smaller pieces if you want more than one colour. And 9 in. of VELCRO, that new hooked nylon fastening more exciting than any zip. It comes in a dozen colours, is $\frac{3}{4}$ in. wide and costs only a few pence an inch.

This compendium is tailored to take up the least possible space without waste, and there are pockets and slots all over, but it folds up compactly into a folder less than $3\frac{1}{4}$ in. x 5 in. So measurements must be accurate. You can, of course,

HOW TO MAKE

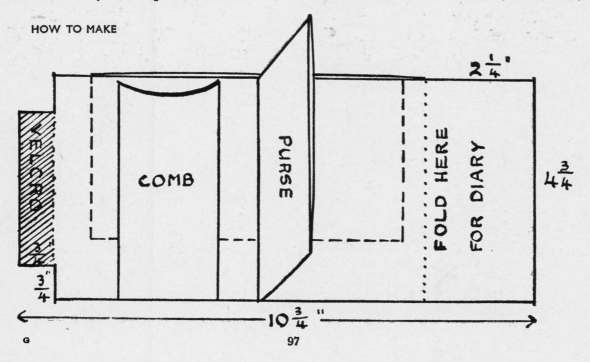

make a roomier one, and in any case you should be ruled by your own individual diary size. This is based on one under 4¼ in. x 3 in.

The diagram will show you the size of the outer felt and the placing of the pockets. The notecase is on the back outer side with safe fastenings. The rainhood out of sight at the back of the comb case.

Having cut your main felt 10¾ in. x 4¾ in., now cut the following. Notecase flap—6½ in. x 3½ in. Purse—6 in. x 4¾

THE FINISHED COMPENDIUM

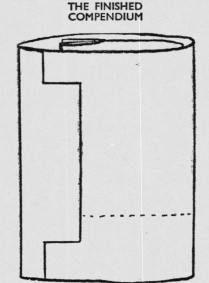

in. This is doubled in two. Comb slot—2 in. x 4¾ in. Rainhood slot—4 in. x 2¼ in. The diary pocket folds back 2¾ in. on itself.

Work in this order using matching cotton and small stitches and where necessary catching the felt only in case you close up a pocket on the reverse side. . . .

1. Stitch notecase in position on back adding two ½ in. strips of VELCRO across the top as fastening.

2. Turn over diary pocket and oversew edges.

3. Stitch up separate purse stitching on VELCRO fastening across opening. Stitch in the fold ¾ in. away from the diary pocket edge.

4. Catch inside comb pocket in position.

5. Catch outside rainhood pocket in position.

6. Stitch VELCRO fastening on tab and felt on outside edge.

7. Oversew all outside edges with strong thread to prevent the felt stretching and to ensure good wearing properties.

The planning takes time, but the sewing is simple and you'll be delighted with your five-in-one compendium.

SOLUTION TO CROSSWORD PUZZLE ON PAGE 53

Across: 1. Shine; 5. Posed; 8. Tan; 9. Via; 10. Rinse; 12. Tango; 15. Area; 16. Gender; 17. Riding; 20. Lasted; 23. Report; 25. Lace; 27. Adorn; 28. Manor; 29. Ewe; 30. Cat; 31. Toyed; 32. Teeth.
Down: 1. Straw; 2. Hair; 3. Inner; 4. Eve; 5. Patent; 6. Sand; 7. Door; 11. Sailor; 13. Angela; 14. Gem; 16. Gist; 18. Darned; 19. Red; 21. Dance; 22. Berth; 23. Rapt; 24. Pony; 26. Coat; 28. Met.

DOUBLE VICTORY

by ARTHUR WATERHOUSE

"CINDY, quick, pass to me!" Cindy Cartwright leaned on her hockey stick and prepared to "roll in" the ball. She saw Della Ames positioned to receive it, then the referee's whistle blew and she rolled the ball straight to her waiting chum.

Della, captain of Ghyll Mere School seniors, made no mistake. She pushed past an opposing player, swerved round her, gathered the ball and dribbled towards the goal circle. Then, dodging another opponent, she hit the ball to Patsy Drew racing in to receive the pass. Patsy steadied herself, smacked the ball hard and true, and next moment a wildly excited crowd of watching girls was yelling ecstatically: "Goal!"

The excitement was made more intense because at that thrilling moment the whistle blew for time. Ghyll Mere had beaten their formidable rivals Green Brow School by three goals to two.

Della ran over to Patsy to congratulate her, and was joined by Cindy running in from the wing. Three happy, smiling girls, now the centre of a milling crowd of players, had manœuvred the downfall of the Green Brow team, captained by the now dispirited Vida Riggs.

It had been a hard-fought game, first one goal up for Green Brow, then a carefully planned second for Ghyll Mere, and finally the winning goal in the last exciting second of play.

"Well, we've done it," chuckled Della gleefully, as the three walked off the field. "That will take the crimp out of Vida Riggs and Company. They didn't think we could win, but I knew that we could. Now for the Inter Schools Tournament, and we'll do it again."

"You bet we will," smiled Patsy. "I don't like crowing, but Green Brow have had the edge on us for two years, and it's time we had a change."

"We can lick them in the swimming events," said Della. "Cindy will see to that, and there's just one more thing I'd like to win——"

Della paused and shot a glance at Cindy, now walking ahead with another player and chatting animatedly. Patsy saw the glance and understood.

"You mean at the gymkhana," she said. Della nodded.

"If only Cindy would join us," she began, then ended on a note of resignation, "But what's the use, she won't even let us talk about it."

"It *is* disappointing," agreed Patsy. "But how's this for an idea? We're the 'tops' just now after our win, so let's ask her to tea and have another shot at chatting her into it."

Della, at the gate of the sports field, said hopefully, "We could try. Perhaps Cindy will be more receptive today. I'd love to win her round into going with us."

Half an hour later the three girls were sitting at tea in Study One at Ghyll Mere School for Girls in Lakeland. The school had once been the mansion of a wealthy cotton merchant, and stood graciously elevated above a velvety green lawn that sloped down to the edge of a lovely lake.

Behind the school towered the great fells that seemed to sprawl away in all directions. Here and there the high peaks reached majestically into the sky, so that at times by night the moon seemed to stand poised and balanced on one black craggy peak like a crescent-shaped lantern faintly lighting the world around.

"Will you have a sausage roll or a meat patty, Cindy?" asked Patsy, moving the plate a little nearer.

"Let Cindy help herself," said Della, filling the teapot with boiling water.

"She is doing," laughed Patsy, as Cindy took a patty. "And do hurry with tea, Della, I'm dying for a cuppa."

Della poured out and passed the tea-cups. Then for the next few minutes conversation almost ceased as three hungry girls did justice to the patties, rolls, and cakes.

Outside spring was on its way. The snow had almost vanished from the fell-tops, and pushing bravely through the fresh brown earth were the crocuses and green shoots of daffodils.

Della swallowed the last of her pastry and glanced significantly at Patsy. Patsy looked towards Cindy and nodded understandingly.

"From this afternoon's play," Della began, addressing herself to Cindy, "we've no need to be afraid of meeting Green Brow again at hockey. And you can take care of the swimming events."

Both Della and Patsy knew that Cindy was a member of a Life Guards' Club at the seaside resort where she lived. And they knew that she had twice received awards for helping bathers in difficulties. Small wonder, then, that she was the "swimmer of the year" at Ghyll Mere. Often she was to be seen practising in the school's reserved portion of the lake, or in the private pool of the Grand View Hotel, which by arrangement the Ghyll Mere girls used.

Now at Della's appraisal of her skill Cindy smiled modestly, and Della continued, "Patsy and I do wish that you'd come riding with us. We could have such fun together, and when the gymkhana comes along we could ride rings round Vida Riggs and Zoe Beck and Company. Gosh, wouldn't it be heaven to do that! You could borrow a hack from the stables, the same as we do."

"You make it sound attractive," said Cindy, indecisively.

"Will you come, then?" exclaimed Della, enthusiastically. "You'd love it, Cindy! It's marvellous riding the valley bridle paths, or following the old pack pony trails over the fells. Patsy and I often wish you were with us when we go off on Saturdays."

Cindy smiled evasively, then, as Patsy tried still further to press her, she looked troubled, her face paled, and she said in a jerky, pained voice: "N-no! I—I couldn't. It's no use your asking." Then followed an embarrassing silence. After

a few moments Cindy pushed back her chair and rose. "I must go now," she said, agitatedly. "I've some prep to do for morning."

"Now what have we done?" asked Patsy, flurried, as the door closed behind Cindy.

"I haven't a clue," said Della, shaking a puzzled head. "There can't be any harm in asking her to join in our riding jaunts. Why is she like that? It's so disappointing. Twice before she's seemed receptive, and then she's suddenly dried up. Now she's done it again. I give up!"

Patsy sat at the table strewn with the soiled teacups and saucers, her face resting in her hands. Her thoughts were following Cindy, now walking swiftly along the corridor outside. It seemed so strange that Cindy should not want to join in their pastime.

Horse riding was all the vogue among

the girls at the Lakeland schools. Some girls even owned their own ponies, but mostly they were borrowed mounts.

Patsy recalled how Miss Smart, the Headmistress, had read them the letter from a local livery stable inviting the girls at Ghyll Mere to take advantage of the wonderful opportunity to see the lovely countryside on horseback.

"I think this is a recreation of which I can whole-heartedly approve," she had said in her immaculate intonation. "Of course, there is the question of fees to be considered. Before any girl hires a horse, I should like the assurance that she can afford to do so, or that any expense will be met by her parents."

Could that be Cindy's reason, the expense? pondered Patsy, as the idea struck home. In her own case she had written to her mother for permission and had received the go-ahead. Della had done the same, she knew. But what of Cindy's parents? How had they reacted?

"I say, Della," she said, "do you think that Cindy's refusal may be on account of the cash?"

Della looked up sharply. "I've been wondering that," she said. "But I didn't like to mention it."

"Well, it could be that, couldn't it?" insisted Patsy.

Della nodded. "If it is she might think we've been unkind to press her."

"But how could we possibly know?" inquired Patsy, a little anxiously.

"How can we find out? That would be a better solution," said Della, in a baffled tone.

"I suppose there's no way of doing that," put in Patsy, defeated. "Just think if Cindy would ride with us, we might win for Ghyll Mere at the gymkhana. We could mop up Green Brow at swimming, beat them at hockey, and I could go home for the hols. quite contented."

Della laughed. "That's asking a lot," she commented.

"Maybe," smiled Patsy, impudently. "But don't forget this is my last term at Ghyll Mere, and I'd like the pleasure of walloping Vida Riggs and Zoe Beck, and any other Green Brow kids who care to come along."

Meanwhile life at Ghyll Mere went its accustomed way. At week-ends while Della and Patsy went riding, Cindy went with other girls rambling and climbing on the fells. Though not an expert, and always taking an easy ascent up a fell-side, Cindy loved to stand on the ridge and let the breeze blow fresh and free around her.

One afternoon as the girls were returning from a ramble Cindy was walking ahead when she saw two riders approaching. Cindy was suddenly seized with a sickly spasm in the pit of her stomach, and turning to the low wall at the roadside she stood there staring out over the wide countryside before her.

Next moment the riders were abreast, and one called out politely:

"Have you seen a boy on a pony along the road?"

Without turning, Cindy replied in a low voice: "No!" The rider muttered something about manners, and the pair clip-clopped away.

"Are you all right, Cindy?" asked one of the girls, coming to her side and noticing her pallor.

"Yes, thank you," said Cindy, trembling, and making an excuse for herself. "My foot hurts a bit, that's all," she fibbed.

The following week-end most of the girls received visits from their parents. At Sunday noon Patsy found herself strolling home from Morning Service at the old creeper-clad local church with Cindy's mother, while her own mother accompanied Cindy and Della.

"Cindy tells me that you are very much looking forward to the annual sports," said Mrs. Cartwright, a pretty, vivacious woman. "She says this term will be your last at Ghyll Mere."

"That's true," admitted Patsy, a little regretfully.

"I believe you are anxious to score off the Green Brow girls before your departure," said Cindy's mother, laughingly. "How like schoolgirls. I remember when I was young we couldn't bear the girls at the rival school to walk off with the prizes. Which particular events are you hoping to win?"

Patsy told her, and explained that if only Cindy would take up riding they might gain a further victory at the gymkhana.

"Why doesn't Cindy go with you?" asked her mother.

The question struck Patsy like a blow. Did it mean that Cindy could go if she wished?

"We don't know," replied Patsy. "We've asked her, but each time she's seemed upset."

"That's strange," remarked Mrs. Cartwright. "I'll have a chat with her. I should have thought she would like to ride."

Later that afternoon, when Cindy and her mother were taking tea in a nearby hotel, Mrs. Cartwright broached the subject.

"Patsy has been telling me that she and Della would like you to go riding with them," she said. "Why don't you go, Cindy?"

Cindy suddenly lost her previous gaiety and went quiet. Her mother saw the colour fade from her face, and asked, "Is something wrong? Don't you feel well?"

"Mummy, I can't go riding," she said, desperately, then went silent.

Her mother waited a while. "You must have some reason, Cindy," she said. "What is it, and why are you so dramatic? It's not like you."

"It's because——" began Cindy, then stopped again.

"Go on, Cindy, please," invited her mother. "If there's something troubling you, then you must let me help."

Cindy, near to tears, burst out, "It's because I'm afraid, Mummy."

"Afraid you'll fall, do you mean?"

"No, it's not that at all," wailed Cindy miserably. "I'm afraid of horses. If I'm out on the road and a rider comes along I'm terrified. I don't know why, but I am."

"I see," said her mother, slowly, realising the seriousness of such trouble in a young girl. "You really shouldn't be like that, but if you are it's a great pity.

Why not try to fight this difficulty—there's no real reason why you should be afraid of a horse. It's only an imaginary fear, you know. Think how horses are among our best dumb friends."

"I know," said Cindy, far from happy, "and I know that you and Daddy both love them, but I can't help myself."

"Well, we'll not bother about it any more just now," said her mother, "so cheer up. Though it does seem a shame to disappoint Della and Patsy—they're such nice girls."

Cindy was only too happy to drop the conversation. Never before had she confessed her fear to anyone, and in bed that night she did wonder what her two chums would have thought if they had

heard her afternoon's outburst. Her mother had said she should try to conquer her fear. How could she do that? Perhaps she *would* like to do so—yes, she thought, she *would*. And she would like to go riding with them; but the next moment her mind wavered as thoughts filled with grave misgivings flooded over her.

As she fell asleep Cindy would have been astonished if she had known what was ahead of her, or even if she had known that Patsy had related to Della what Mrs. Cartwright had said about her refusal to go riding.

Then, one sunny afternoon in early summer, Cindy was taking a solitary walk along the path by the lake shore. Gazing into the distance, she could see a boat moving slowly over the water. The afternoon was beautifully clear and Cindy could easily discern the splash of oars as they dipped into the lake. Not another boat or person was in sight.

Cindy turned her gaze from the lake to the peaceful landscape. About fifty yards ahead was a low stone wall running down to the lake path, and in the field beyond some cattle grazed. Cindy noticed a brown pony standing with its head over the wall, and apparently watching her approach.

Cindy quailed as it moved down the wallside nearer to the path.

Now what should she do? Cindy didn't know that the pony was used to being fed pieces of sweet apple by a girl

like herself, and that it was now hoping for another tit-bit.

At that moment a loud scream pierced the silence. Cindy's glance flashed in the direction, and in alarm she saw that the boat had somehow upset, and that two people were struggling in the water. Instinctively Cindy knew that she must help them, and began running forward. Then with a start she realised that if she ran all the way she would be breathless, and in no state to swim out to the boat. What *could* she do?

The pony was now almost on the lake path. Without further thought Cindy ran to it, led it beside the wall and scrambled on to its back. Then, seizing its mane, she clung on and dug in her heels. Turning it towards the scene of impending disaster, she urged it on.

The pony knew what to do, and, breaking into a fast trot, it was soon pounding in a flat-out gallop along the lake shore. At a spot opposite to the capsized boat Cindy, never realising what she had just done, leapt from the pony's back, rushed into the water and struck out.

Swimming strongly, she was soon alongside. There, two girls were in real difficulties. One clung desperately to the upturned boat, while the other bravely attempted to right it, and at the same time tried to console her badly frightened friend.

"Can you swim?" Cindy asked the second girl.

"Yes," she spluttered, shaking water from her head.

"Then strike out for the shore," ordered Cindy. "I'll bring your friend along." To the first girl she said, as she pulled her away from the boat: "Do as I tell you, and don't struggle, then we'll both be safe."

The girl's frightened eyes wavered in understanding, but she never spoke, so Cindy turned her onto her back, took a firm grip on her, and struck out for the shore. Cindy thought that swim would never end, but at last the three girls stood dripping water and shaking on the grassy lake edge.

"We'd better go home and change," said Cindy, as the other two smiled weakly and thanked her. "You look like Green Brow girls."

"We are," said one, "and you're from Ghyll Mere," she added, noticing Cindy's school uniform. "It's a good thing you were on hand."

The pony now walked up and pushed its head between the three. Cindy patted its rough neck. "You should thank this pony, too," she said. "If it hadn't been near I don't know what might have happened. It certainly helped in the rescue."

Then it struck Cindy with terrific force

that she had actually ridden it, and the shock of the realisation set her trembling violently. A Green Brow girl noticed, and misinterpreting the cause said with concern, "Let's be going, we shall all catch cold."

Hurrying home, Cindy thought of what she had done. She felt happy and amazed at the same time. The rescue was prompted by her Life Guards training, but the pony ride—that was something she had never expected to do. Now, instinctively, she knew that never again would she be afraid of a horse. That one ride, she felt sure, made in perilous emergency, had cured her fear for ever. The more she thought of her hasty action, the more she knew it had won for her a wonderful victory.

When she reached Ghyll Mere she dashed straight to Della's room. She and Patsy were preparing tea.

"Hello, Cindy, you're just in time," said Patsy, then noticing her soaked clothes she asked in alarm, "Whatever have you been doing? Have you been in the lake?"

"Yes, I have," cried Cindy, excitedly, "but never mind about that. I've done it, that's what I want to tell you."

"Done what?" exclaimed her astonished friends.

"I've ridden a horse," cried Cindy, jubilantly. "It's the first time, ever. I was afraid before, that's why I wouldn't go with you. Now I won't be afraid any more. Isn't it marvellous! Oh, I'm so happy!"

Patsy and Della stood wide-eyed with amazement as Cindy's story bubbled out. Then as it ended and the two listeners stood beaming with delight, Della said joyously, "Now we'll *all* go riding."

"And now for a Ghyll Mere victory over Green Brow at the gymkhana," added Patsy. "Hurry up and change into some dry things, and we'll have a real celebration tea party."

The next day when the headmistress of Green Brow telephoned to thank Cindy for helping her two girls from probable disaster, and Cindy was praised before all the school, she instantly became the hero of the hour.

After that the three chums began attending riding school together. Cindy, with the encouragement of Della and Patsy, took to the saddle like a fledgling to the wing. And by high summer, when the gymkhana took place, Cindy could ride sufficiently well to join the Ghyll Mere girls in the different events.

Already Ghyll Mere had won the annual hockey match, and with Cindy performing like a water sprite in the swimming pool the aquatic honours were a further laurel.

At last came the great day. On a sunny morning Della, Patsy, and Cindy presented themselves at the stables to collect their mounts.

Della and Patsy were given the horses they usually rode, but Cindy was informed that a Green Brow girl had been given in mistake the one that she had ridden. Cindy was terribly disappointed and upset at the news.

"Don't worry, miss," said the proprietor, cheerfully, "I've got another one just as good. I've only had this pony a couple of days, and consequently none of you girls have ridden him. But the farmer who sold him told me he's quiet and a grand ride. Here he is, miss," he grinned, as a stableman led a bright-eyed chestnut pony into the yard.

Cindy looked at it, and caught her breath. "Why, you darling," she cried, running to him.

Della and Patsy stared in amazement. They had shared Cindy's disappointment of a moment ago, and now they were at a loss to understand her sudden turnabout. Cindy's next words explained her joy.

"This is the horse I rode by the lake that afternoon," she explained, fondling him. "Help me up, please," she requested the stableman eagerly.

Soon three happy girls were riding from the yard. Della and Patsy had ridden their mounts many times, and went calmly along, but Cindy was so elated that somehow she transmitted it to her pony, and he with tossing mane and flashing eyes almost danced down the road towards the gymkhana field.

Quite a lot of spectators and competitors had arrived when the three chums rode into the field. At the stewards' tent they received their number cards, and were asked to wait in the collecting ring. Meanwhile, in the middle of the grassy arena a band played a gay tune.

Vida Riggs and company were already there. "Hello," she greeted Della and Patsy. "I hope you're unlucky today." Zoe Beck giggled at the quip.

"Thanks," said Della sweetly, "I hope we are . . ." then ended with crushing emphasis, "NOT", and as she rode over to the hitching rail she called back: "See you in the ring, soon, Vida!"

A number of locals were there with smart-looking ponies, and the Ghyll Mere girls realised that it was not going to be easy to win any of the events.

The jumping prizes were all captured by youthful members of Young Farmers' Clubs, and then the novelty races began. Vida Riggs had soon won the Ball and Bucket Race. The riders had to race out to a row of wooden buckets, and each had to pick up and deposit half a dozen balls in one of the buckets while holding on to their mount, and then race back with the bucket to the winning post. That made Green Brow one up on Ghyll Mere.

Then followed an event that went to a local rider. After that came the amusing Washing Day Race. Each rider was given a bundle of dry washing and some clothes-pegs. They had to race to a clothes-line strung up at one end of the field, hang out their washing, and race for home.

As the line was purposely stretched fairly high most of the riders had to stand in the stirrups to reach it, and if the pony moved they could not manage to peg out the garments, and then the fun began.

One boy was so eager that he over-balanced, clutched at the line for support and dragged it down, causing much confusion to the riders, and much laughter among the spectators as nightgowns, shirts, and aprons fluttered gaily to the ground.

But Patsy was lucky. She was at one end of the line and her portion didn't drop so much, so she was able to finish her pegging out and race home the first, to Ghyll Mere's advantage. The two schools were now "one all".

Next came the Sack Race, which Zoe Beck easily won by being the only runner not to fall. Two to one now in Green Brow's favour.

Both schools failed at the Relay Race. But in the Blindfold Race Della reached the winning-post first, mainly due to her lucky avoidance of the bumping and jostling of the other riders. Now the rival schools were two each, and only the Musical Chairs event remained.

"We must win this," said Patsy, as the Ghyll Mere girls waited to enter the arena.

"You bet we shall try," said Della, "but it's more good luck than anything else, this time."

Cindy, half laughing and half serious, said: "I've got my fingers crossed, and this pony was my good friend before, so perhaps if I give him a pat for luck he'll help me again. There," she said, smiling, as she patted his neck, "just you be in front of a chair when that band stops playing."

"Come on," said Della nervously, "they're waiting for us. They've put the chairs ready."

Eleven riders trotted out into the arena and took up starting positions beside the ten chairs. Then the band struck up. Round the line of chairs trotted the ponies, and one by one as the music stopped the riders were eliminated. Patsy lost her place, then Zoe Beck, then Della, and when it got down to the last two Cindy excitedly saw that she had to battle it out with Vida Riggs. On the result of this last ride rested the deciding score for the two rival schools.

One solitary chair stood challengingly in the middle of the green field.

The two girls sat their mounts in tense excitement. Then the band played and the riders moved off cautiously, both trying hard to describe the smallest possible circle round the chair.

Round and round they went, and still the band played on. Then as both girls were positioned equally in front of the chair it suddenly stopped. Like a flash the riders slipped from the saddles.

Vida Riggs in the backward position snatched at the chair. But at that moment a small piece of paper blowing across the field whisked before her pony's eyes.

The pony jerked its head away, and in that split second Vida, unexpectedly tugged sideways, missed her grasp on the chair and it fell rolling to Cindy's feet. She swooped down, grabbed it, and, setting it upright, firmly sat on it.

Across the field streamed the excited Ghyll Mere girls to congratulate Cindy. Della and Patsy, thrilled and delighted, slapped her on the back.

Then came the Green Brow girls to acknowledge their defeat. Vida Riggs, barely concealing her annoyance at having had victory so unluckily snatched away, offered her congratulations with a poor grace, but the Ghyll Mere girls were so excited that they hardly noticed.

Patsy said a few moments later: "Now I'm really happy. I shall remember this summer as our year of victory."

"I shall remember it," said Cindy happily, as they rode from the field, "as my year of double victory. I conquered my fear, and I helped the school to win."

Della said: "Gook luck to Ghyll Mere. Our wishes came true."

JENNY ON HER OWN

Jenny had been a probationer nurse at St. Olave's Hospital for four months. Now she was in real trouble. "Show more initiative, Nurse!" said the Matron.

"But, Mary," wailed Jenny as she prepared to go home for her one off-duty night a week, "how *can* I show initiative? You see nothing ever happens!"

When Jenny Marlow got off the bus to walk the last mile or so to her home she was very thoughtful. "If ONLY something would happen!" she said to herself. "Then I could——" She stopped as there came a cry for help. It was very faint but was quite unmistakable.

"Help! HELP!" came that cry again.

In a moment the young nurse raced towards the cliff edge. But her heart thudded with fear, real genuine fear!

Reaching the cliff edge, a scared Jenny peered over. "Oh, NOOO!" she groaned. "I—I can't! I—I must fetch help."
But she knew that would be too late.

"P-please help me," groaned a boy of about twelve. "I—I think I have broken my leg. You can climb down quite easily. PLEASE!" But Jenny hesitated.

"Don't move!" she called out. "Whatever you do, DON'T move your leg. I'll fetch help." "No! Please don't leave me!" screamed the boy.

"All right," called out Jenny at last. "I'm coming." Then she thought: "This WOULD happen. The only thing I'm scared of is heights. The ONLY thing!" Yet she started that terrible climb downwards towards the injured boy. "I'm a nurse," she kept telling herself, "and a nurse mustn't be afraid. EVER!"

"Don't look down, Jenny," came from the injured boy whom she knew quite well; "you must look upwards. Oh, hurry! HURRY! I—I think I'm going to faint!"

Then the boy DID faint. But, somehow or other, the probationer nurse reached him at last. "Thank goodness!" she whispered. "There is a length of rope!"

So Jenny attended to her first real patient, and even the Matron of St. Olave's Hospital could have found no fault with the way she handled things.

Now the boy was comfortable, Jenny soon attracted the attention of some holiday-makers on the sands far below. "HOSPITAL! QUICKLY!" she cried.

It was a long wait until police and an ambulance arrived, but Jenny was the perfect nurse to her patient. "You did SPLENDIDLY, Nurse!" declared a doctor from the hospital. "I couldn't have done it better myself. Don't let anyone tell YOU that you haven't any initiative. You'll make a good nurse, my dear, a very good one."

The YOUNG SPINSTER

by PHILIP M. PETHICK

As the train steamed out, Philippa Winster stood on the country station platform and stared up and down its short length. The suitcase in her right hand was heavy and the hold-all in her left none too light.

"What do I do now?" she muttered to herself. "Someone will meet you, Auntie said, but who?"

The only person she could see was a uniformed man at the barrier. He was quite likely stationmaster, porter, ticket collector, and everything else of the tiny place. Philippa moved towards him just as a young girl of perhaps seventeen, dressed in a cotton sweater and jeans, walked through the barrier and onto the platform.

Philippa's hopes rose. Was this the person who was to meet her? If so, the Easter holidays might not be so bad after all. To spend them with strangers was bad enough, but if one of them was a girl only a year or so older it made the outlook a deal brighter.

"Excuse me," the new arrival said, moving towards Philippa, "did anyone else get off the train with you—an elderly lady?"

"No. I was the only one," Philippa answered, her hopes sinking rapidly. What a shame the girl had come to meet someone else. She looked such a cheerful, merry person, even though she was now frowning with annoyance.

"I thought this would happen! Trust an old dear to get the wrong train. That means I've got to come back this evening."

And with that the girl turned about and strode away through the barrier. A second or so later there came the sound of a motor-car engine from behind the station building. Philippa hurried to the barrier and stared out into the sun-drenched yard. She was just in time to see a red sports car swirl away, puthering dust out from its rear wheels.

"Ticket, miss?"

Philippa dropped her case and fumbled in the little pocket of her costume coat. She had not lost the ticket, so that was something!

"How far is it to Bannock?" she asked.

"Five mile, miss! Next village along the road to the right out there."

"I was going to be met here, but I can't see anyone. Could I get a taxi or a bus?"

The elderly man chuckled. "No taxi in this place, miss! The bus don't run Tuesdays and I got to shut the station up now. No train till after tea and I've other things to do. Best get into the yard there and wait. Your folks'll come, I reckon!"

And so for a quarter of an hour Philippa sat on her upturned suitcase and became more miserable with the passing of each minute. The sun poured down with a warmth that was unusual for spring, and the only person she could see was a small boy slouching against the open yard gate. He bobbed out of sight when she called to him.

She might as well have been in a deserted village for all the signs of activity she could see. Not a soul stirred in the cottages scattered haphazardly away from the station. And even that was unoccupied now, for the elderly fellow had slammed the door shut and later she had seen him ambling away down the line.

"The telephone! What an idiot!" Philippa suddenly cried aloud and jumped to her feet.

There in a corner of the yard was a red kiosk. She hurried across to it,

pulled open the door and gasped from the blast of heat that swept out at her. She just could not stay inside with the door shut, the over-strong spring of which had crashed it to after her.

"Well, take the directory outside!" she told herself aloud, but that was chained to the wall.

There was nothing for it but to thumb over the pages with the book on the shelf designed for it, whilst she held the door open a little with one foot.

"I knew it!" she growled in exasperation. "There's not a Burton in Bannock! Why, there are no B's at all! The pages are torn out! This is the limit!"

From the corner of her eye she saw a movement outside the kiosk. It was the small boy from the gate, staring through the glass wall at her.

"I bet you tore these pages out!" she muttered, frowning fiercely at him, then forgetting him as the roar of an engine made her swing round. The door shut quickly, trapping her ankle. She cried out in pain and anger, feeling tears well up in her eyes.

"Why on earth did Auntie have to do this to me?" she stormed, freeing her ankle and tumbling out of the kiosk.

Then she realised that that was very mean on her part, for Aunt Clara was not responsible for having to rush off to Scotland to nurse a sister suddenly taken ill. And, as she had explained to Philippa, she was a true sister and quite alone.

"But I know of some people in Bannock who run a guest-house. They say they'll be pleased to have you for Easter and it's not so far from your school as coming to London," she had said on the telephone only yesterday. That had been when Philippa had been called to the headmistress's study on the last day of term, to take the call from her aunt.

"No, I can't blame Auntie, I suppose," Philippa muttered, looking down at her ankle. "She's certainly done all she could for me since Mummy and Daddy had to go to Australia. It'll be fine when I've finished with school and can go out there to them."

Having had her few seconds of self-pity, Philippa looked around to see what had caused the noise. Just where she had left her case stood a motor lorry. The driver had got down from the cab and was surveying something on the ground by the front wheels.

"Oh no!" Philippa squeaked and ran across the yard, her costume coat flapping open, her wavy hair flying back from her head. "Not my case!"

"'Fraid so, miss!" the driver grunted as she slithered to a stop beside him. "Never saw it until too late!"

The left front wheel had caught the suitcase and sprung it open. Her school uniform had shot out to the dusty ground, but that had acted in some measure as a protection to more delicate items of clothing, now spilled on top of it.

Philippa sank onto the step of the lorry, plumped her elbows on her knees and buried her face in her hands. For a few seconds she would have burst into tears if the lorry driver had said a word. Luckily he was too embarrassed. Finally she looked up and the sight of his blushing face was too much. She simply burst out laughing.

"Miss! What is it?" he gasped out, taking a step towards her, then becoming even more confused. He stopped and stared at his grimy hands held before him for some reason.

"Oh, just the last straw!" Philippa cried out, getting to her feet. "No one's met me, I'm locked out of the station, I can't telephone, I've trapped my ankle in the kiosk door, and my luggage is flattened! If I didn't laugh, I'd cry!"

"Say, I'm sorry, miss. Let me give you a hand with your clothes. No, I'd better not. My hands aren't clean."

Philippa swept the clothes together and banged the case shut. It would not fasten, of course, but the lorry driver was dangling a length of rope before her, saying: "I can rope it round for you, any-way! Where are you wanting to get to?"

"Bannock. The Burton Guest House there. Fancy a place like that in a village. Do you know it?"

"I know of it, miss. I don't come from these parts. I work for a construction company. We're building a new factory about two miles from here, but I've heard say there's good fishing at Bannock."

"Oh no! Don't say I've got to spend Easter with a lot of old fishermen!"

"Young people fish, but I can't say I like it. But look—I'll give you a lift part of the way and whatever damage is done to your things, send the bill to my boss."

"That'll get you into trouble, won't it?" Philippa asked as she watched the man put her now battered suitcase and holdall into the cab.

"Not as much as being caught giving you a ride, miss! It's against the rules. Can't even take me young son around with me, 'though the nipper tries to get aboard often without me knowing it. But I'm giving you a lift, so get up into the cab. Just got to get some crates of glass from the station first!"

"It's locked up! The only man looking after it I saw walking away along the line."

The lorry driver muttered something under his breath, then went on a tour of the station. He returned empty-handed and climbed into the cab where Philippa was already sitting.

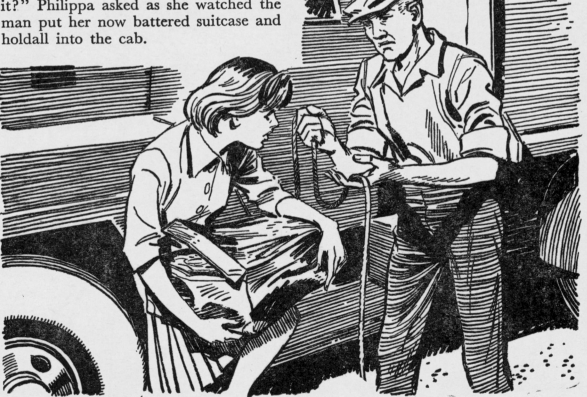

"You were right. No one about. What a cock-eyed place this is. Fancy building a factory out in the wilds like this! Now I'll have to come back this evening, I suppose!" he growled and started up the engine.

They moved out of the yard and turned right along a narrow road, soon leaving the scattered cottages behind. It was a noisy, bumpy ride, but much better than walking with her cases in the heat of the sun.

Two miles soon passed, and after taking a sharp bend the lorry slowed to a halt, some twenty yards or so before a large break in the left-hand hedge. There the ditch had been bridged and the rutted, cut-up grass verge showed only too plainly how lorry after lorry had gone through the gap. A field away, Philippa could see the lower storey of some great concrete and steel building in the course of erection.

"'Fraid you'll have to get out here, miss!" the driver said. "Just can't take you any farther. The site boss is lodging in Bannock—maybe he'll be heading that way for lunch. You just walk on a bit and see if you can get a hitch."

Philippa thanked him, climbed from the cab and took her cases as they were handed out. Dumping these on the grass verge, she stood back to let the lorry move on. This it did with a jerk, the engine nearly stopping. As the rear of the lorry drew level with her, a dirty, cheeky face peeped over the top of the dropside. It was the boy from the station yard again.

He was clearly alarmed at seeing Philippa and half stood up in surprise. At that moment the lorry engine picked up and the vehicle bounded forward. The little urchin was flung off balance and came rolling over the tailboard, fighting to get a grip and break his fall.

"Oh no!" Philippa gasped, her hands

coming up to her face in a gesture of horror.

The lorry was some feet from her now, with the boy clinging desperately to the tailboard. It was a forlorn hope and another jerk dislodged him. He fell almost head first to the road and lay still.

Philippa shouted, but the lorry driver had no chance of hearing her over the sound of the engine, so she stumbled forward to help the boy. Before she could reach him, Philippa heard the car coming round the bend. A quick glance over her shoulder showed her a red sports model travelling fast, bearing down on the urchin, who had now staggered to his feet.

But he was dazed and floundered to the centre of the road. The driver of the car saw him, but, confused by the boy's erratic steps, swerved the wrong way. Philippa shrieked at the top of her voice, then flung herself forward across the road in front of the car and at the boy.

There was no time to stop and pull him back. She plunged on, swept into him, gathered him in her arms and fell to the road. Over and over Philippa and the boy rolled. In one split second she saw the front wheels of the car almost upon her head. Tyres shrieked in her ears, dust sprayed over her, then she felt grass around her and she and the boy were falling. They hit the bottom of the ditch and lay still.

And all was quiet! No car or lorry engine sounded! Philippa disentangled herself from the urchin. His grimy, frightened face stared up at her from the ditch bottom, but there was no sign of pain in it.

"You're right enough!" she muttered, scrambling out of the ditch and only then realising how she was trembling from the reaction to her narrow escape. "But what of the car driver?"

The car was in the opposite ditch, a few yards from the long break in the hedge to the factory buildings. Only the rear of it was visible, and only one wheel of that. This was off the grass, then touching the grass, then clear of it again.

"It's just balancing!" Philippa gasped. "The driver's trying to get out! He'll have it over on top of himself!"

She scorched across the road, forgetting her trembling limbs and shortness of breath. The car was just on the brink of the deep ditch, ready any second to roll over and crush the driver dazedly trying to scramble out from under the steering-wheel.

"Keep still!" Philippa shrieked. "It'll go over!"

As she grabbed the rear of the car and flung her weight upon it to keep it down to the ground, she saw that the driver was not a man. It was the girl of the sweater and jeans.

"My foot's jammed under the pedals!" the girl gasped out, forcing a grin to her lips.

"Can't help you—it'll turn over if I let go!" Philippa gasped.

"You stay there then! I'll get out!"

"Don't struggle—someone's coming!" Philippa had seen a figure running through the gap in the hedge. It was the lorry driver, so he had heard her shouts or something. Then, out of the corner of her eyes, she noticed a small figure sprint across the road towards the man. It was the muddy-faced cause of it all and he flung himself at the man with a wild cry of "Daddy!"

"Help! Quick!" Philippa yelled, seeing that the man was going to start a cross-examination of the boy.

The lorry driver looked up, took in the situation instantly and bounded forward to the sports car.

"You, miss!" he gasped, but was looking at the girl in the driver's seat, not Philippa.

"My foot's trapped!" the girl answered.

"The car's tipping over, you idiot!" Philippa shrieked at the man in desperation.

"I can see that!" the man snapped back. "Can you hold on a minute or so? Got to hold it back somehow."

"Yes, but hurry!"

He was off in a wild run, through the gap in the hedge, ignoring the little boy standing rather stupidly there. Philippa heard the lorry start up and its electric horn blowing. In a few seconds it appeared on the road, the horn still blasting the air as a call for more help. It roared by her, then reversed until only a few feet away. A chain slammed and clanked behind her, but she dared not look round for fear of letting go of the car.

"Hang on a few seconds more, miss!" the lorry driver's voice muttered behind her as he fumbled with the chain under the car. "Got it fixed! I'll take up the slack, then you hop clear as I pull her out."

He sprinted back to the cab, the horn started blasting its call for aid again, then the engine of the lorry roared. The chain tautened beside Philippa's feet and the sports car came down hard on the ground. As it started to move backwards out of the ditch, Philippa levered herself off the car and staggered clear. Then, before the lorry driver could get back to them, she had the door of the sports car open and was gently prising the girl's foot from under the pedals. It came free quite easily and she helped her stagger from the car.

"I daren't lean to the left to get free," the girl gasped. "Oh gee! Thanks a lot! I think I'll sit down!"

"I'm going to lie down!" Philippa muttered and lowered herself to the grass, flopping back full length and sighing with relief. She was trembling in every limb now, her lips and throat dry. She closed her eyes.

"What the blazes was all that hooting, Stevens?" a voice demanded somewhere above her, but for the moment Philippa was not bothered, even when it went on.

"And, Janice! Your car! Stevens—your boy! The chains! What's happened, man? Who's this girl?"

Philippa heard the lorry driver, obviously named Stevens, answer: "Don't know, sir, but she's just saved my nipper's life and your daughter's, most likely! 'Fraid I gave her a lift from the station. She got out just here, then as I turned into the field, I saw, through the mirror, my nipper staggering about in the road behind me!"

"Fell off the lorry back, eh? The times I've warned you about him!" the other voice growled.

"Yes, sir! Anyway, your daughter's car was heading straight for my lad. Not her fault, sir! She came round the

bend and there he was. Then the girl I'd just put down flung herself across the road and carried my nipper with her into the ditch over there!"

"Great Scott!" the other voice gasped out. "Then Janice ended in this ditch, missing them both?"

"She missed 'em right enough, but when I'd stopped and got back here, the car was tipping over, with your daughter trapped. This other girl was hanging on like fury and keeping it down. I've just dragged the lot of 'em out!"

"Seems we both owe her a lot," the voice muttered. "Guess she's fainted."

"No I've not!" Philippa retorted, stung by the remark. "But how I'd like to get to the Bannock Guest House without something else happening!"

A quarter of an hour later she was

there, driven by Mr. Franklin, the father of Janice, and the lorry driver's employer, in his car. Little was said during the trip, except that Janice explained that she and her father were lodging at the Guest House during the building of the factory.

That news cheered Philippa immensely, and the sight of the trim, white-walled building in the centre of a really charming village almost brought her spirits back to normal. But she was in for yet another shock.

In the entrance hall of the Guest House they were met by the owner, Mrs. Burton, a kind-looking, cheery, middle-aged woman. Janice's father introduced Philippa by saying: "Another of your guests, Mrs. Burton, but I'm afraid the old lady hasn't arrived yet. That's so, Janice, isn't it?"

"Yes. She must have missed the train. I got there just after it had gone, but she couldn't have had time to get off the platform. Why, Philippa here hadn't even given up her ticket. Pity I didn't ask you where *you* were going. 'Fraid I was a little mad at having to meet the old lady, to be honest, even though I volunteered to do it."

"Just a minute," Mrs. Burton said with a worried frown. "I've only one extra guest booked for Easter. I'm sorry, my dear, but I know nothing of you coming here. What with the fishermen, Mr. Franklin and his daughter here, and others from the factory buildings, I'm full up!"

Philippa slumped down on her battered suitcase in misery and disgust. The thing immediately burst the rope around it and spilled its contents and Philippa onto the floor. Everyone jumped to help her and haul her to her feet.

"Just like Auntie Clara!" was all Philippa said in a weary voice, then after a pause went on, "I bet it was some other village she phoned yesterday and told me this one!"

"Did you say Clara?" Mrs. Burton asked. "Would that be Clara Masters?"

"Why yes! That's Auntie's name. Then she did phone yesterday!" Philippa gasped.

"My old school friend Clara Masters telephoned right enough. The line was bad, crackling, but I did hear her say that a Miss Phillips wanted a room—an elderly lady I judged, a spinster. That's why I asked Janice if she'd meet her with her car."

Philippa suddenly burst out laughing, crying out: "Everything's all right! I'm your guest! Auntie said 'Miss Phillips— a spinster' you think?"

"I'm sure she did—her very words!"

"No, Mrs. Burton! I'm sure she really said 'Miss Philippa Winster' — that's me!"

And as the explanation became apparent, there was laughter from all, and it sparked off the best three weeks' holiday Philippa had ever had—and her friendship with Janice Franklin!